The girl in the room is Hilary's maid. Or is it Walter's maid? The other maid is gone for the day and so is the cook. This maid in the room is the younger one, a robust girl who paints her face before she visits the market. Hilary is certain that one day she saw the maid in the rue de Vaugirard with a pair of sailors.

In any case the maid's face is not painted now. Maybe a touch of rouge on the lips but not more than that. The girl's name is Therese and Walter has her bent over one of the smaller tables in the room with the light streaming in from that open window to cast a halo over each head.

Walter's head and the maid's head.

He presses behind her, his body bent over hers, his left hand extended. The maid's blouse is undone and her left breast hangs out like a ripe melon into Walter's extended hand.

CAROUSEL

DANIEL VIAN

BLUE MOON BOOKS
NEW YORK

Published by
Blue Moon Books
841 Broadway, Fourth Floor
New York, NY 10003

ISBN 1-56201-123-5

Manufactured in the United States of America

PART ONE

Dancing Mad

The mouth first. The lips are slightly apart, the lower lip showing more of the red lipstick and a hint of wetness over the surface.

The face is tilted, the face of the woman tilted upwards, her cheeks flushed and her eyes almost closed.

Not everything is revealed in the first instant. The doorway shows only part of the room, the window, the afternoon light streaming in from the right, the shutters pushed out a bit to allow the light and the warm air to penetrate the indoor space. We see part of the room and then we see part of the corridor outside the room. The corridor is dark, unlit by any windows, the walls a dull brown color and any sounds in the corridor muffled by the carpet that extends along the floor.

And then suddenly the view shifts and pulls back and then again we see the woman who stands in the corridor, the woman standing there with her eyes on the doorway that leads into the room, standing there as far back as the wall of the corridor, back in the shadows in the corridor, not completely in the frame of the doorway, just enough in the frame so that she sees no more than a part of the room.

The face is tilted, the face of the woman tilted upwards, her cheeks flushed and her eyes almost closed.

The woman is young, a young woman with dark hair cut short in the fashion of the day, a narrow knee-length dress and grey stockings and soft leather shoes with a low Louis heel. She has both hands at her sides, her eyes fixed on the doorway that shows the interior of the room, just part of the room revealed now in the frame of the doorway.

Her name is Hilary, a young woman also known as Mrs. Walter Blair. Her face is tilted, Hilary's face tilted upwards, her cheeks flushed and her eyes almost closed.

But Hilary moves a bit further to the right and now she sees more directly into the sunlit room. Bright sun, a shaft of bright sun coming in from the right side of the room to illuminate the interior and the two people in the room who remain motionless and who show no awareness of the presence of Hilary in the corridor.

A church bell sounds the hour. One strike of the bell. One strike to announce the time and to punctuate this first moment. One strike from the church of Saint-Sulpice as Hilary stands there in the corridor with her eyes on the interior of the room.

The corridor is stuffy, too warm to be comfortable, the air thick at one o'clock in the afternoon. Hilary moves now, a slow movement that carries her body backwards until she leans against the wall. She feels weak. She wants to move again but she remains immobile. She's afraid to move again because her presence might be revealed. She wants to be motionless. Hilary, don't move. She wants to be motionless as she looks into the room to watch them.

The girl in the room is Hilary's maid. Or is it Walter's maid? The other maid is gone for the day and so is the cook. This maid in the room is the younger one, a robust girl who paints her face before she visits the market. Hilary is certain that one day she saw the maid in the rue de Vaugirard with a pair of sailors.

In any case the maid's face is not painted now. Maybe a touch of rouge on the lips but not more than that. The girl's name is Therese and Walter has her bent over one of the smaller tables in the room with the light streaming in from that open window to cast a halo over each head.

Walter's head and the maid's head.

He presses behind her, his body bent over hers, his left hand extended. The maid's blouse is undone and her left breast hangs out like a ripe melon into Walter's extended hand.

One full breast hanging like a ripe melon.

Hilary closes her eyes.

Then the maid groans and Hilary opens her eyes again. Hilary moves just an inch more to the right to obtain a better view of things. Her eyes are locked on Walter's hand, the hand that holds the maid's breast.

My husband's hand, Hilary thinks.

Something is happening now. Walter is moving his other hand, his right hand, the hand hidden by his body. He's pulling at the maid's clothes, pulling at her skirt, raising it, unveiling her plump thighs, her broad rump.

Therese is naked under the black skirt she wears, completely naked above the gartered black stockings. What a miracle it is to have the girl's white buttocks suddenly shining like that in the afternoon sunlight. Walter's right hand is moving again and Hilary knows where it is. She has a glimpse of it now. The maid's quim. The maid giggles as she feels Walter's fingers in her quim. The word explodes inside Hilary's head. The maid's quim. Walter's fingers in the maid's quim. No artifice, Hilary. It's a quim, all right. Only partly exposed when the girl is bent over like this, but exposed enough to show the dark bush of hair between the girl's legs, that dark furry thing between the milk-white thighs and below the rounds of her buttocks.

Walter is fumbling again. Oh yes, Hilary thinks. Hilary trembles as she watches the appearance of Walter's organ. In all fairness he looks quite potent. Eager and quite potent. Hilary is trembling again. Someone is laughing in the street, down at the front of that awful restaurant where the waiter was once so rude to Hilary. Only once. She won't set foot in the place any more. There's no such thing as a good restaurant on Boulevard Raspail. It's nothing but smelly soup and grime these days and Walter won't listen to her when she presses him to take a flat somewhere else, at least in a quiet district where they won't have the motorcars and the gasoline fumes and the poules of the Boulevard under their noses.

The maid is groaning again. Hilary has avoided the business for no more than a moment, and now she's forced to be attentive again, to watch them, to watch the pushing of Walter's organ into the maid's exposed sex.

I'm his wife, Hilary thinks.

She's unable to stop watching them, unable to turn her eyes away, and of course as Walter pushes forward it occurs to Hilary that the fact that she's Walter's wife is at the moment quite irrelevant to the two people in the room.

Walter has now completed his penetration of the maid's grotto. Hilary thinks of it as a grotto, a dark place, dark in the maid and dark in herself, dark and wet in the maid no doubt, dark and receptive, dark and warm as it holds the penetrating member. Hilary keeps her eyes on the coupling, the joining, the pink organ protruding now, revealed for an instant and then concealed again.

Nothing hidden, Hilary thinks. Everything is so completely exposed. The maid, Walter, the maid making a sound in her throat as Walter pushes against her, Walter's organ moving slowly, his left hand still extended to clutch at the girl's heavy breast.

He does as he pleases. Hilary knows Walter well enough to understand that at this moment he does as he pleases. None of that feigned uncertainty he always displays. At this moment Walter has his organ sliding in a wet cave and he does as he pleases. Hilary wonders what he has in his mind as he pushes himself in and out of the maid's affair. Does he imagine things? The sunlight has sharpened a bit now, increased its brightness and shifted just enough to emphasize even more the maid's hairy attributes.

The girl groans again. Hilary stares at them. She glances at the open window and she stares at the coupling again. Walter is moving with more determination now, a quickening conveyed at once to the maid whose groans are now more frequent, the pitch a bit higher as the ending arrives.

The arrival. They arrive. Hilary is transfixed as she watches it. The attainment of the crisis. Is it the maid or is it Walter who arrives first? Hilary hears the grunting now. Walter's grunting. Her husband grunting. Well, it doesn't matter, does it? He grunts the same when it's Hilary who's at the end of it. You wouldn't think one of the Boston Blairs would grunt like that, but there it is. It's not at all lyrical, not at all a pleasant sound. The grunting in the room, the window open, the maid moaning now as she wiggles her hips.

The bloody bastard, Hilary thinks. The bloody, bloody bastard.

* * *

This is a wall, a garden somewhere, perhaps in the Grenelle district. The man and the young woman are separated by no more than two meters. The man is dressed in a dark suit, a vest, a white shirt with a stiff collar, a tie, a peaked cap. He leans forward, his right arm stretched out towards the woman, his left hand holding one part of his jacket that is now unbuttoned and hanging open at his waist.

The young woman has her back turned to the man, her back turned no more than two meters away from the man, her left arm raised, her head turned slightly to the left as if she has just glanced at the man behind her, just

glanced at him over her left shoulder. The young woman
wears a blue silk dress, the hem at mid-calf, blue kid
shoes and blue silk stockings. Her left leg is bent, the toe
of her shoe pointing at the ground, pointing at a small pot
of flowers that has just been overturned by her foot.

Now the young woman moves again, her left leg
moves, her left foot, her body, her face turning away
from the man again as she moves forward.

The man leans forward a bit more as he reaches out to
the retreating woman, as he reaches out without stepping
forward, as he reaches out to the young woman who hurries now to the far end of the small garden.

—Marceline!

A frightened bird suddenly flutters out of the shelter of
a small tree.

* * *

In a taxi now, Hilary sits in the back corner closest to
the sidewalk in the rue de Rennes. The taxi is not moving; the pedestrians on the sidewalk seem immobilized as
Hilary slowly crosses her left leg over her right knee, as
she slowly turns her head to once again stare at the
streaked glass that separates her from the silent driver.

She trembles. She stares at the street again, at the
pedestrians who are now moving slowly past the cab
while the cab itself is motionless in the traffic of the
boulevard. She feels the knot of anger again. All these
people on the sidewalk seem so content with themselves.
What an awful thing it is not to be as content as these
people. Oh Hilary, what a fool you are. You must be
more cunning about things.

She thinks of Walter's expression, the pleasure on his
face as he fondled the maid, the twisted agony as he
finally arrived. She hasn't seen his face like that in a long
time, not since that wild night on the *Aquitania* as they

left the harbor in New York. Walter was drunk on champagne and he insisted he wanted to look at her as they made love. She remembers his twisted features now, his lips pulled back against his teeth, the look of hot madness in his eyes.

The taxi driver curses at something in French. Hilary's French is good enough so that she feels an immediate annoyance. She glances at the seat beside her and for the first time she notices the stains on the leather. A feeling of revulsion sweeps over her as she considers who the previous passengers might have been. Some Parisian slut and her paramour, the woman wetting herself as the man fondled her breasts in the rear of a taxi.

As wet as the maid, no doubt. Hilary recalls the little scene again, Therese the maid bent over the small table in the room with her fat breast in Walter's hand and her fat rump pushing back at Walter's belly. She'll have to go, Hilary thinks. She couldn't bear to have the maid in the flat now. The girl must leave immediately. Oh Walter, I despise you. That little tart with her breast bared, the dark nipple so luscious as Walter squeezed it with his fingertips.

My marriage, Hilary thinks. My marriage died in the bush of one of my maids. What an awful thing to see it like that. But not all of it, really. With Walter at the girl like that, most of the essentials had been hidden, no more than a glimpse of the girl's hairy sex as he stroked in and out with such impatience. He wouldn't dream that Hilary might return unannounced, just a moment in the flat before she continued on to an appointment with her dressmaker. Like a tawdry joke, Hilary thinks: Finding himself alone with the maid, the errant husband presses his advantage, presses his Boston pickle into the maid's Gallic pudendum.

Damn you, Walter.

The taxi is moving again, turning right into the

Boulevard Saint-Germain, turning past the church and
into the traffic towards Odeon. Hilary gazes at the street
with such an empty feeling in her chest. The knot of
anger is gone and all she feels is a great nothingness. She
has a sudden memory of a sound, one of the sounds they
made in the room. Did she imagine it? No, she did not
imagine it. Now for the first time she clearly remembers
that sucking sound, the sound of Walter's organ moving
in the girl's grotto. What an awful ugly sound it is, all
that wetness, that awful little tart dripping all over
Walter. Is it true the French girls are always in rut for it?

But I do love Paris, Hilary thinks. She tells herself that
after all it's not the maid's fault, it's Walter's fault. How
ignoble of him to take advantage of a poor servant.

Hilary sighs. She uncrosses her legs and immediately
recrosses them with now the right leg crossed over her
left knee. She tugs at the hem of her skirt to cover her
right knee. She glances down at her right foot, twists her
ankle as she examines her shoe.

Then she looks at the window again, at the pedestrians
on the sidewalk. Her eyes move from one pedestrian to
another. She does like to look at people. She loves the
crowded streets, the men and women strolling in the
afternoon.

But not this way, she thinks. Not sitting here on the
soiled bench of a taxi, the driver smoking and the smoke
drifting back to mix with the gasoline fumes and the
smell of Lord knows what in the dank interior of the cab.
Hilary looks at the soiled leather again and she suddenly
wishes she could pluck herself out of this taxi and into a
garden somewhere, a quiet cloister where she might rest
her nerves.

Curiosity calls. Hilary slowly extends her left hand, her
fingers moving slowly over the leather of the seat to find
the place where the leather is soiled. She rubs her fingertips over the dark spot. She thinks of Walter again, how

different it was for them in New York. His people came down from Boston and they weren't that pleased about the marriage.

Dear God, I'm perspiring, Hilary thinks. She can feel the dampness of her skin. A shudder passes through her as she remembers Walter in the room. The grunting. His mouth gaping.

The taxi slows and stops and then moves on again.

Hilary feels a quiver of excitement. A shiver passes through her as once again she remembers the scene in the room. Then she feels a rebellion against the same excitement. She feels something pulling at her. She pictures the maid again, the girl's rump thrust out, the girl's hairy sex exposed. And other bodies. Hilary shudders as a rippling mass of white flesh undulates through her mind. Younger girls; pubescent girls; secret memories. Then Walter again. His face, the stupid look in his eyes as he fondled and stroked the maid. How awful it is. But I'm not a child, Hilary thinks. She imagines herself to be a mature woman. She's not a child, after all. Yet why does she quiver when she thinks of the coupling, the sliding, that sucking sound made by the girl's wet sex as it gripped Walter's penis?

Dear God, I'm wet, Hilary thinks. Yes she is. She crosses her legs again and she can feel the wetness.

* * *

This is a café near the Opera, in the foreground a man and a woman seated at a table, in the background the other patrons of the crowded café, one man standing with his left hand on his hip and his head turned as he gazes at the cluster of tables.

The two people in the foreground, the man and the woman, sit facing each other, the woman's legs crossed, her left elbow on the table and her left hand holding a glass, her right hand on her hip, her eyes on her companion. The man sits leaning forward a bit, his head inclined forward, a glass in his right hand, the white collar of his shirt stiff against a fold in his neck.

The man has white hair and he must be past sixty. The woman is younger, a woman of thirty with a mass of dark curls piled on her head, a heart-shaped face with a spot of rouge on each cheek, the décolleté of her blouse showing the upper slopes of her breasts, her legs covered by dark silk and the hem of her peach-colored skirt pulled back far enough to show the crossing of her knees and the charming curves of her calves.

Now the man moves. He moves his left hand along the top of the table and he touches his right elbow with his fingertips as he lifts the glass to complete the journey to his mouth.

The woman does not move. She remains motionless as she smiles at the man.

—You're not a foreigner.

—No, the man says.

—I don't mind the foreigners, but I'd rather be with my own kind, eh?

* * *

The dressmaker smiles at Hilary. The window is open and the warm air floats in from the rue de la Baume. Hilary stands before a long mirror with her eyes on her image, on this new dress that clings so tightly to her hips and thighs. It's a black dress, a fine tulle evening dress with a long waist.

The dressmaker is a woman of forty with dark eyes and red lips.

—The sequins are charming, madame.

Hilary nods.

—Yes, I think so.

She wonders what Walter is doing at this very moment. Is he at the maid again? Yes, why not? Perhaps at this moment he has the maid on his lap in the sitting room.

Hilary studies her new dress. She wants to escape. The dressmaker smiles again as she moves from one side to the other to consider the fit of the dress at Hilary's shoulders. The door to the small fitting room is open, a murmuring audible from the workshop down at the end of the corridor. Hilary is aware of the dressmaker's eyes on her body. She feels a dull apathy again as the dressmaker's fingers tug at her shoulders. The dressmaker pulls at the dress to tighten the fit at the bust a bit. Hilary watches the dressmaker in the mirror, her eyes on the dressmaker's hands, on the dressmaker's throat that appears so pale above the blue of her corsage.

Now Hilary feels a sudden anger again as she remembers the maid's plump breast hanging into Walter's caressing palm. She keeps her eyes on the dressmaker, on the dressmaker's throat. Hilary suddenly wonders if the dressmaker looks old when she's naked. Does she have drooping breasts? Madame Valois. Hilary wonders what Madame Valois is like with her lovers. She imagines Madame Valois groaning on a bed somewhere. Or perhaps Madame Valois admits her lovers into the fitting rooms in order to have the jousting as convenient as possible. In the fitting rooms, no doubt. And now Hilary feels the dressmaker's hands again and Hilary quivers. Madame Valois is running her fingers along Hilary's waist and down to Hilary's hips. The dressmaker murmurs something but Hilary hears none of it. Hilary feels the fingertips stroking her hips, tugging at the material of the dress, tightening the fit. The dressmaker is complimenting the shape of Hilary's bottom and Hilary tells herself that yes, it's a definite flirtation. She hasn't lived in Paris two years for nothing. She feels a sudden heat in her face. The room is much too hot. The mirror wavers

*

in front of her. Hilary quivers again. Don't be an idiot, she thinks. She takes a deep breath. Hilary, don't confuse your capabilities. Madame Valois is chattering about the dress again. The dressmaker's fingers are now stroking Hilary's bottom and Hilary shudders again.

Hilary turns, contains her annoyance.

—How soon can you have it ready for me?

—One week.

—That's fine, then.

—Let me pin it now.

The mirror again, Hilary's eyes on her own face, on her mouth and throat. Now in her mind there is nothing but the scene in the room, the sliding of Walter's organ, each stroke so definite, his face so clear in the sunlight, the excitement in his face, his hips pushing forward and retreating and pushing forward again, the grunting, the bestial grunting at the finish.

Oh Walter.

Hilary trembles again as she imagines a flood of sperm inundating the maid's grotto. Hilary, it's only a maid. It's a marriage and it's only a maid.

He enjoyed it. His balls were full and he did enjoy it.

Darling, it's a problem, isn't it?

Her eyes on the dressmaker's mirror, Hilary gazes at her own face as she quivers again.

* * *

This is one edge of la place de l'Opéra, the cabriolets and the broughams and an occasional bicycle maneuvering and sounding their klaxons to avoid each other, and in the midst of the confusion of motorcars the pedestrians hurrying from sidewalk to sidewalk. In the distance is the huge opera house, the winged figures at each corner standing like sentinels over the bustle in the square, the huge dome glittering in the bright sun, the stone figure atop the dome with its arms raised to the heavens with an offering and a supplication.

The traffic moves in a jerking circle, a jerking movement from one edge of the square to the other, an erratic shifting of the motorcars, a laugh, a klaxon calling, a laugh again as the movement continues.

This is Paris in the year 1925.

2.

Is it Monday? Monday noon near the Bourse. Boom boom. You can hear the construction in the Boulevard Haussmann. Here is Monsieur Gazan in his office in the rue St. Joseph. He stands in his shirtsleeves, both hands raised, his eyes on his desk. He seems harried. His desk is cluttered with papers. All that trouble in Morocco. The fools. Well, what do you expect? They don't know anything. Idiots in the ministries. The franc isn't worth a damn anymore and it's getting worse. They pull their moustaches. It's too much, isn't it? We're all suffering from shell-shock. The war is over but now it's the shell-shock. People with rotting minds signing one decree after another. Bleeding the Boche. Oh, they don't mind bleeding the Boche if they can catch a few drops for their own pockets. Ha ha. Get their pockets wet, won't they?

The telephone rings. Two quick rings. Monsieur Gazan turns to face it, looks at it, and then lifts the receiver.

—Hello?

Now a woman's voice.

—Monsieur Gazan?

—Yes.

—This is your friend in the rue Rossini.

—Oh, yes.

—We have someone new. A lovely girl. Good family. She's exquisite. I thought you might be interested.

—When?

—At three o'clock if you'd like.

—Fine. Yes, that's fine. I'll be there at three.

* * *

The music is clear, the trilling of a cornet, the sound of it clear and sharp a full moment before anything is visible. Then the cornet trills again and a light suddenly appears that illuminates the immense marble hall, the painted ceilings, the glass floor over which are scattered a hundred small tables, each table occupied, each table isolated and in its own space away from the other tables surrounding it. A rectangular dance floor can be seen in the center of the huge room, and at the far end the brilliantly lit green water of a swimming pool surrounded on three sides by twenty fountains that continuously pour water into the air, the fountains dropping and rising and dropping again, the entire aqueous ballet accompanied now by the music of a Neapolitan guitar band ensconced in one of the small balconies close to the painted ceilings.

Hilary and Walter and some of Walter's friends sit at one of the small tables near the center of the hall.

—Well, it's divine, Walter says with a laugh. The Lido is always divine.

Yes, the Lido is divine. Walter smiles at his friends, at Arthur and his French girl Gaby, at Jack and his girl Michelle, at Hilary as she sips her champagne, at the other tables, at the dance floor. Walter's Harvard chums. Hilary despises the French girls, these bubbling little tarts with dark eyes and red lips and breasts vibrating like mounds of jelly under their silk dresses. Everyone talks, talking and laughing, toasting each other for one silly reason after another.

Jack flirts with Hilary. The two French girls wiggle
their shoulders and giggle at each other. Jack smiles at
Hilary, his eyes on her throat, her shoulders, the swell of
her breasts, her bare arms, the smooth white skin of her
arms.

Jazz music now; a jazz band has replaced the Neapolitan guitar band on the small balcony. The people at the
tables raise their hands to applaud. Arthur calls out to
Hilary:

—Don't you love Paris?

—Yes of course.

—It's a party, isn't it? It's a long party.

—Yes. A long party.

Hilary quivers. All these creatures in this great hall.
The fountains at the edge of the pool are rising again.
Jack leans over to whisper something to Hilary, but she
hears hardly any of it and in any case it doesn't matter.
She can tell by his eyes what he wants. Does Walter
care? Walter seems absorbed in Jack's girl, the blonde
Gaby. Jack dares to run his fingertips over Hilary's wrist.
He smiles. He winks. Hilary shudders but she does not
move her wrist away. Jack is a man of independent
means. Arthur is a man of independent means. Walter is
a man of independent means. Now the talk is interrupted
again as a dozen dancing girls run out on the dance floor
with a great show of pink ostrich feathers. The men at the
table begin babbling about the Harvard-Yale game in the
fall. Everyone must go; everyone must return to America
for the most fabulous party. Walter laughs, an emphatic
laugh as he tells a story about the game the previous season. Hilary is bored. She watches as Walter amuses himself. My husband. This enormous party of French and
Americans. This dungeon. Yes, this is her dungeon. Have
some more champagne, Hilary. At least drink the champagne in your dismal dungeon.

Dancing now. Kaleidoscopic shafts of light, now

purple, now blue, now orange, projected on the dance
floor from somewhere above their heads, above the heads
of the people milling about as they move towards the
arena. Walter is off with one of the French girls and Jack
takes Hilary's arm. A thin man with rolling eyes taps his
feet rhythmically at the edge of the raised dance floor.
Hilary dances with Jack. She gazes at the gleam of bare
backs as Jack continues his flirtation with her. The fox-
trot music goes on and on, the music embellishing the
rustling sounds of short skirts, the gigglings, the whisper-
ings, the occasional gasp. Hilary wonders if her legs look
attractive. She feels dizzy, overwhelmed by the constant
hum of laughter and small talk.

Then she dances with Arthur. Another bout of the fox-
trot. Walter is still dancing with one of the French girls.
The lights are changing again. Jack returns to sweep
Hilary away from Arthur. Hilary has a glimpse of Walter
whispering in Gaby's ear. The memory comes to Hilary
now: Walter and the maid. Walter and the girl Therese in
that room. Walter poking the maid with such gusto in the
bright light of the afternoon sun that streams into the
small room. Hilary shudders. Jack laughs. He kisses her
neck and Hilary shudders again.

* * *

Silence. The nightclub party is only a memory now as
Walter mumbles something in the silence of the Blair
bedroom.

Hilary and Walter are at home, Hilary's thoughts are
interrupted as she tries to hear what Walter is saying.

—Did you say something?

—I said I'd like more champagne.

—Well, have it if you like.

—I will. You don't think I drink too much, do you,
darling?

Hilary watches as he opens a small bottle of champagne. She wonders if the servants are asleep. Or perhaps the servants are listening to them, their ears against the walls or the floor or whatever it is that servants do.

Walter talks again.

—Don't you think Jack and Arthur are swell?

—Yes, of course.

Walter reviews the evening of piquant pleasantries. He talks about Paris. Dear God, he never stops talking about Paris. Talking about Paris is such exhausting work these days. Hilary removes her jewelry. She strokes her chin with her fingertips. She contemplates her boredom. I'm so bored. What an awful thing it is to be bored. She gazes at her image in the mirror, at the gentle slope of her breasts under the silk of her evening dress. She recalls the instant when Jack kissed her neck, the feel of his lips on her neck, the feel of his wet lips.

Walter sits on the bed. This is Hilary's bed. Walter's bed is in the adjoining room. He sits on the bed with his glass of champagne in one hand and he smiles at Hilary and calls her to him. Yes, she goes to him. She leaves the mirror to sit on her bed with her husband.

After draining his glass of champagne, Walter carefully places the empty glass on the nightstand. Then he smiles at Hilary again and he leans forward to kiss her. He holds her face in his hands as he kisses her. He whispers something, but Hilary can't make it out. She tells herself it doesn't matter anyhow since everything that follows is predictable, all the moves predictable, all the moves exactly known.

A kiss again as they sit there on the bed beside each other. He's drunk; she knows very well he's drunk and she hates him for it. The most difficult thing in the world is to love an intoxicated Boston man. The Blairs of Boston. Hilary hates them all. His snorting uncles, his dried-up aunts, the dust of the dreary generations clouding their eyes. Walter is looking at her legs and thighs now, at the white flesh above the tops of her stockings where the dress has been pulled back by the awkward way he has her sitting on the bed. She expects the inevitable now, the ultimate physical invasion that always brings her more trouble than pleasure. She feels his arms around her body. He seems so pleased with himself. He kisses her again, her neck, perhaps the same spot where Jack kissed her in the nightclub. In her mind she compares the two kisses, the kiss of her husband and Jack's kiss. Walter is chuckling about something. Is he talking about his chums again? She prays he might ask her if she feels tired. For the first time she notices that his shirt has been tossed away. His arms are bare, his chest covered by an undershirt, his arms moving as he strokes her knees, his eyes on her bare thighs.

And now the doing of it. Hilary has her eyes closed as she lies back on the bed. Her dress is gone, everything gone except her stockings and the pink suspender belt, her eyes closed and her head turned to the side and one leg raised high in the air as Walter presses himself upon her, as Walter presses his turgid organ into the quick of her sex, his belly against the underside of her right thigh, her right leg raised and somehow pushed to the side so that her calf presses against his right shoulder, Walter grunting now as he slides himself in and out of her sex, as he pushes and pulls, as he strokes his organ with a series of jerks, a pause, and then a series of jerks again.

Does Hilary feel any pleasure? It's not obvious. Her eyes are closed, her mouth hanging open a bit. Her right arm is raised so that her right hand rests on Walter's left elbow. But Hilary's hand is not clutching at Walter's arm. There is no objective sign of pleasure as Walter continues his penetration, as Hilary is penetrated by Walter's thrusting organ, as Walter grunts and slides his belly against the underside of Hilary's right thigh, as

Walter now grunts again and finally obtains his release, and finally spurts his liquor into the interior of Hilary's pummeled sex with a final grunt and a final wriggle and a final intoxicated shuddering.

* * *

Is there any pleasure in it? Hilary lies in the dark and she tells herself it doesn't matter. She has her satisfactions. There are severe days and there are delightful days and she has her satisfactions. There are doors that must not be opened. One must not ring the bells of certain doors. She tells herself she doesn't care. She can't imagine her dearest friends are any different. Now she's angry again as she thinks of Walter's betrayal with their silly maid. Hilary remembers how the girl moaned. The question is whether or not Hilary has ever moaned like that with Walter. Well, have you? she thinks. She doesn't know. I don't know. A shudder passes through her as she recalls the pressure of Walter's thrusting organ. She tells herself she doesn't understand it. She tells herself she doesn't understand the meaning of it.

* * *

This is Hilary at the age of eight. She sits near a window. She wears a white dress with lace frills that hang over each shoulder. Under the dress she wears a dark blouse with long sleeves. She has long hair, the hair parted in the center, the hair framing her face to her shoulders in front and flowing down over her back. Part of the flowing hair can be seen over her left shoulder, behind the lace frill.

She holds an open book in her hands, but she's not looking at it. She holds the book with both hands. The light from the window is bright on Hilary's right side, on the book, on her white dress.

This is the year 1908. Is it spring or summer? The
window is closed and the few branches of the tree that
can be seen through the window are still without leaves.
It must be spring. March or April in the year 1908.

* * *

In the breakfast room, Hilary smiles at Walter as he
puts his newspaper down.
—Darling, I think we ought to find some new servants.
Walter stares at her.
—New servants?
—The maids are becoming sloppy. I'll have the agency
send some girls around. You don't mind, do you?
—Is it really necessary?
—Yes, I think so.
—Hilary, this is Paris. All the maids are sloppy in
Paris. Let's wait until the end of summer, shall we? The
fall is always a better time. We'll give the maids notice in
the fall, if you like, but I don't think you'll find any girls
better than those we have now.
Then he mumbles something about lunch with Jack and
he turns to look at the window.

* * *

Hilary keeps her eyes on the maid Therese. At occasional moments she finds Therese and Walter whispering
at each other. One warm afternoon towards the end of
May, Hilary notices the satisfaction in the girl's face.
My maid, Hilary thinks. She hates Walter for it. She
hates him more and more for it.
She continues to watch Therese. The girl's mouth is too
luscious. Hilary remembers the moaning again, Therese
moaning as Walter pushed against her from behind. The
girl had so much enthusiasm. Hilary watches the maid as
the girl glides fom one room to another with her dark

eyes bright and lovely.

They have a hunger for it, Hilary thinks. The girls of this type have a hunger for it. Hilary feels annoyance again. She tells herself she ought not to be obsessed by it. The absorption is morbid. Damn Walter and the maid. The girl has such a full rump, so white and smooth when it's illuminated by the sun.

My own existence, Hilary thinks. It's not Walter or the maid, it's my own existence.

In any case, she knows all about Walter. Hilary understands him. He's a Brahmin, isn't he? Despite all the comforts, he's vaguely dissatisfied. He feels constrained by conventions. There are men who do not like an ordered existence. Is that why he married her against the wishes of his family? Oh Walter, you're so confused. Hilary feels a sudden sympathy for him. And then the sympathy is once again replaced by a violent hatred. She closes her eyes and once again she sees the maid bending, the rump of the maid pushing against Walter's belly, Walter pushing back, Walter groaning as he pushes against the maid's broad behind.

* * *

Boulangerie.
Pâtisserie.
Epicerie.
Parfumerie.
Hilary is following the maid along the Boulevard Raspail. What a little bitch the girl is. What bad luck it is to have brought her into the flat to play the temptress to Walter.

Hilary, you're imagining things. It's not the girl's fault, it's Walter's fault. It's not the maid, it's Walter.

Hilary follows the maid at ten yards. She's thankful for the crowd on the boulevard, the pedestrians doing their

errands in the afternoon air. Therese continues walking
with a definite determination. Hilary watches one stupid
face another as they pass her. Could they possibly imagine that she's following her own maid? Hilary hears the
horns of the motorcars. A flock of pigeons moves from
one rooftop to another rooftop. Oh, the madness of it,
Hilary thinks. She wonders what she looks like. Does
she have the look of madness in her eyes? The pigeons
are flying again. They whirl from one side of the
boulevard to the other in a total confusion.

Then on the other side of rue Péguy, Therese suddenly
turns to vanish into a doorway. A small hotel, the windows covered by green raffia blinds. Hilary hurries to the
entrance, the saliva now gathering in her mouth. Therese
is gone, no one but an old desk clerk ready to sleep
again. He nods at Hilary and shows his yellow teeth.
Hilary speaks in a casual tone.

—That girl. . .
—Madame?
—Has she taken a room?
—A room has already been taken by a gentleman.
—I want a room next to theirs.

Hilary extracts a hundred-franc note from her purse.
The old clerk is pleased. For a hundred francs she'll get
more than just an adjoining room. He shows nothing in
his face as he nods and takes the money. Does he have
the vaguest idea of things? Hilary follows him up the narrow staircase, the creaking steps to the second landing.
He leads her into an empty room. I'm Walter's wife,
Hilary thinks. Anyone ought to understand it. The old
clerk is pointing at something, and when Hilary follows
his finger she sees the peephole.

She stands there lost in thought. The old man turns and
shuffles away and leaves the room and closes the door
behind him.

A moment of silence. Hilary trembles in a moment of silence.

*   *   *

Through the peephole. The room has only one window and the raffia blind has been lowered, but the afternoon light is still strong.

Walter and Therese are standing near the bed. Walter's face is hidden, his head bent as he buries his face against Therese's right shoulder. The girl's head is thrown back and her mouth is open as if she's moaning, but no sound is heard, not any sound at all. Walter's right hand has the girl's dress raised almost to her hip, enough to uncover the white skin of her left thigh and below that the top of the black stocking rolled over the binding garter.

Therese's left leg is pushing forward between Walter's thighs. The maid has her left hand pressed against the front of Walter's trousers, her fingers gripping his penis through the cloth.

Now they move. A murmuring, nothing but a faint murmuring. Walter sits on the edge of the bed and he watches Therese as she begins to undress. The girl smiles at him as she removes her blouse and her skirt. She wears a white cotton brassiere and white cotton drawers. She teases Walter by turning her back to him as she pushes the drawers down her legs and off her feet and then bends to retrieve them.

Hilary sees everything. A shudder of frenzy passes through Hilary as she watches Therese reach behind with her hands to pull her buttocks apart in front of Walter's face.

A bubbling laugh from Therese now. The girl unhooks her brassiere and drops it onto a nearby chair. Then she turns to Walter and she leans over his face to push one of her plump breasts into his mouth.

Walter sucks at the dark nipple. Hilary can see his

mouth working, his lips moving as he sucks at the teat.

Walter's right hand moves over Therese's belly and he slowly slides his fingers through the bush of dark hair between Therese's white thighs.

They move again. Walter is now half-leaning on the bed and Therese has shifted her body so that her back is seen more clearly by Hilary, her back and her buttocks and her thighs. The girl lifts her left leg to push her knee at Walter's chest and the dark hairy canyon of the girl's sex is suddenly exposed to Hilary's eyes.

Hilary stares at Therese's fleshy rump, at Therese's round buttocks, at the dark split between the white cheeks, at the aggressive bulge of the girl's sex.

Hilary can see the fingers in Therese's quim. Walter's fingers. Walter pushing his fingers inside the girl's quim.

Then the fingers are pulled away and in a moment Walter's right hand reappears to slide over Therese's left buttock and clutch at it.

Therese laughs and shifts her body backwards. She lowers herself, lowers herself to the floor on her knees with her hands working at the front of Walter's trousers, her fingers working as Walter mutters something, as she giggles again, as she finally bends her head to his lap.

Hilary sees nothing except the girl's head moving up and down and the girl's buttocks like a pair of white moons above the girl's heels. Walter's head is bent, his eyes on the head in his lap, his mouth open and his eyes almost closed.

Then Therese pulls away and Walter quickly undresses himself. They hurry now. The girl wipes her mouth as she waits for him. In a moment Walter is at her, the two bodies naked on the bed, Walter forcing the girl to bend over with her rump in the air, his hands gripping her fleshy hips as he drives his organ into the dark cave of her sex.

Hilary watches it. She watches it to the end, and when

Walter is finally grunting in the other room, grunting as
he drains himself into the girl's receptive body, Hilary
pulls back from the wall and she falls onto the bed behind
her and she suddenly begins to cry.

A quiet crying. Hilary's hand covers her mouth and the
sound is muffled, a quiet sound, a sound of quiet sobbing.

* * *

There are two men standing near the end of the bridge
at the Quay de Conti. They wear dark wool jackets and
baggy grey trousers and old black shoes. One of them
stares at the river. The other takes a curved pipe out of
his mouth.

—What do you think?
—Think about what?
—Morocco.
—I don't care about Morocco. Let them have it. Let
them have the camels. That's a stinking beast, isn't it?
Ugly face. You can smell them at the zoo. Who the hell
cares about Morocco?

3.

Monsieur Gazan is having tea with Madame M. They
sit in a room in the rue Rossini, two chairs, a small table
between the two chairs, two teacups and a teapot on a
tray on the table.

They are not looking at each other.

Madame M. still wears her cloche hat, which indicates
she may have just entered from the outside. Madame M.
sits with her legs crossed and her face turned away from
Monsieur Gazan. She has her eyes on a woman who is
standing near the door, a tall woman who also wears a

cloche hat. This woman wears black gloves and she has a cigarette in her mouth, a long white cigarette dangling from her red lips.

Monsieur Gazan does not look at either of the women.

Madame M. nods at the other woman, and now the woman with the cigarette turns and she leaves the room.

Madame M. turns to face Monsieur Gazan. She uncrosses her legs and then she crosses them again as Monsieur Gazan shifts his body in his chair to look at her.

Madame M. smiles.

—So you want Marceline again?

Monsieur Gazan shrugs.

—Yes, why not?

—She's a darling, isn't she?

—Is that her real name?

Madame M. chuckles.

—Yes, that's her real name. But I won't tell you anything more about her. I've already told you too much. It's not fair, is it? I want the girls to feel safe here. She's a lovely girl, isn't she?

—Yes, quite lovely.

—Not too shy. It's not good when they're too shy. I suppose some men like it, but that's not what you want, is it? You don't want them too shy.

Monsieur Gazan shifts in his chair.

—No, not at all.

* * *

Someone is shouting in the rue La Boetie, shouting down from a window somewhere, a woman's voice rising and then diminishing and then finally there is nothing but the coughing sound of a black taxicab rolling towards the place St. Augustin with a trail of blue smoke curling out of its rear exhaust pipe.

Hilary sits in front of a café with her friend Vita.
Hilary frowns at the noise of the motorcars in the street.
She wishes the café was in a park somewhere. Vita seems
to enjoy the bustling in the street and on the sidewalks.
Vita has a wide red mouth and fine English skin. Now
there's a flurry of sparrows over their heads and Vita
laughs.

—It's a lovely afternoon, isn't it?

—Yes, Hilary says.

But she feels a disintegration in her belly. She tells herself she can't be more unhappy than she is at this
moment. She notices a pair of whores near the entrance
of a corner bar. The women stand there with their eyes
on every man that passes. Hilary wonders about the
poules. She wonders about her marriage, about conse-
quences.

Vita signals the waiter. She wants a glass of wine.

—I'd rather have wine than coffee, Vita says to Hilary.

The other tables are occupied by men, younger men
and older men, all of them pretending to be men of
affairs, occasionally glancing at Hilary and Vita, then
glancing away to study a motorcar in the crowded road.

Hilary looks at her friend. Vita's husband is at the Brit-
ish Embassy. Vita always seems so certain of things, so
unmoved by dislocations and discomforts. Hilary wonders
whether to confide or not to confide. She does need to
talk to someone. She's always thinking about Walter and
the maid and her mind is out of breath with her thinking.
She wants a bit of hope again. Hope for what, Hilary?
What sort of hope is it that you want? She refuses to
admit how awful she feels. I won't admit it, she thinks.
She wonders if Vita has her secrets. She wonders if Vita
really approves of her. Maybe she doesn't approve. What
sort of life does Vita have?

—I need your counsel, Hilary says.

Vita smiles, the red mouth wide and smiling.

—Counsel, darling? What sort of counsel?

—It's about Walter.

—Oh dear.

Hilary confides. She tells everything. That first discovery of Walter and the maid. Does it sound banal? She talks about her problems with Walter. The revelations pour out one after the other. Vita listens with an occasional twitch of her wide mouth, an occasional hint of amusement.

—It's awful, Hilary says.

—Darling, it's not as awful as you think.

—It's not the sort of marriage I ever wanted.

Vita smiles.

—We don't always know what we want. Does Walter know that you know?

—Not yet.

More questions. Hilary hates it. She tells herself she wants to die. She looks at Vita's eyes to guess what Vita is thinking. Hilary trembles. She rambles as she talks about Walter. It's not fair, Hilary thinks. It's not just. I ought to have justice in this. How awful of him to choose a maid. She remembers the scene again, Walter grunting as he finished. And the rendezvous in that dreary little hotel.

—There was also another time, Hilary says.

—Tell me, darling.

Hilary tells all, the maid in the boulevard, the small hotel, the bribing of the hotel clerk, the peeping.

—He was at her in the other room.

Vita laughs.

—Well, yes of course, I should think so.

—It's not amusing.

—Yes, you're quite right.

But Vita's eyes show a contradiction. And now Vita reaches out to touch Hilary's hand and Vita smiles. Once again Hilary is aware of the loveliness of Vita's complexion.

—I'll try to help you, Vita says.

Help her? How will she help her? Vita seems more amused than shocked by Hilary's troubles. The bloody bastard, Hilary thinks. She hates Walter more than ever now. He's brought her to this. How awful the amusement in Vita's eyes.

—I'll help you, Vita says again. Come along with me now and you'll see.

* * *

So they leave the café at last. Hilary grimaces at a beggar on the sidewalk, a dancing clown with torn trousers. She climbs into a taxi with Vita and now Vita is talking about the summer season in Deauville. Vita says she loves the tables, the gambling. Something special, you know. Vita pulls at the hem of her skirt, fidgets on the taxi seat. Hilary wonders where she's being led. Vita snickers when she's asked. Into what little hole in Paris is Vita leading her? Vita has a passion for excess. Too much of everything, Hilary thinks. But here I am. It serves me right for talking about my troubles. One shouldn't talk. It's better not to talk at all. Vita chatters about London. She loves her seasons. She says she has her own pleasures. Husband Charles has his own pleasures and Vita has her own pleasures and everyone is quite happy thank you.

Along the Boulevard Italiens now. What a frenzy it is, what frenetic intensity. Construction in the Boulevard Haussmann. A detour. The taxi finally turns into a narrow street off rue Laffitte and in a few moments Hilary follows Vita into a passage where Vita finds a huge brass knocker and an ancient door that opens immediately as the knocker is slammed down by Vita's hand just once. A maid smiles at them. They pass into a dark interior.

Hilary glances about her as she attempts to discover
where she is. But she can't make it out. She finds the draperies atrocious. She can't make it out, but whatever it is
it's an establishment of some sort. Discrete, yes? Oh yes,
discrete, Vita says in a whisper, her eyes laughing at
Hilary. Just a moment of patience, darling. We'll have
some fun, won't we?

A woman of fifty appears, a gesturing creature
enveloped in a cloud of perfume. Madame Mathilde. The
dark eyes dance as she exchanges pleasantries with Vita
and smiles at Hilary and waves her fingers at their noses
and rolls her eyes at the walls in maroon silk and patches
of Empire gold fleur-de-lis. Flower-de-Luce. The center
piece so much like a phallus. Hilary quivers. She has an
inkling now, a quivering inkling of where she is, where
Vita has brought her. Oh, how nasty Vita is. Hilary
avoids the eyes of the Frenchwoman. Hilary pretends
she's in some sort of trance. Or perhaps the trance is real
after all. How can she stand on the carpet in a place like
this without a barricade of some kind? It's awful. The
carpet is so deep. Fleur-de-lis on the walls and the deep
red carpets. Vita takes Hilary's hand and Hilary finds herself being led along to a staircase, more carpet on the
steps, so many steps, and then a silent corridor and a
door sliding open without a sound and now the interior of
a small room, the light so dim the room is almost in darkness. Madame Mathilde raises a finger to the rosebud
pout of her lips to caution them as she approaches one of
the walls, as she pulls at a small knob, as she slides a
panel slowly to the right.

Hilary trembles. She wants to flee. But Vita still holds
Hilary's hand and now Vita pulls Hilary foward. The slit
that shows the adjoining room is wide enough so that
both Vita and Hilary can stand side by side and look
together. Madame Mathilde chuckles softly and pulls back
with a rustling of her silk dress, a quiet retreat, a careful

closing of the door behind her. Vita smiles at Hilary and
squeezes Hilary's hand and Hilary feels the heat in her
face and the trembling in her legs as she wonders how it's
possible for Vita to be so playful about this.

A girl enters the adjoining room.

The girl is perhaps twenty, a slender girl with short
dark hair and a lovely swan-like neck and a narrow blue
dress with an accordion-pleated skirt that floats about her
knees. She sits down on a velvet-covered bench with her
eyes on the closed door. In a moment the door opens and
a man enters, a boulevardier with a small dark moustache
and pink cheeks and a quick movement of his legs as he
closes the door and then steps toward the girl.

Hilary is mesmerized as she watches the man and the
girl mumble at each other, the man standing, the girl still
sitting, the man close enough to the girl so that she has to
bend her lovely neck backwards in order to look up at his
face. Is the girl smiling? The girl now lowers her head as
she raises her right hand to touch the front of the man's
trousers.

Vita squeezes Hilary's hand.

The girl unbuttons the man's flies, one button after the
other, no hurry in the doing of it, and then she slips her
slender hand inside the gap of his trousers, fumbles a bit
and finally extracts a limber and surprisingly long penis.

Limber and long. Hilary is surprised by the length of
it. He's not at all a tall man and yet he has such a long
penis. Limber and long and thick in the girl's hand.
Hilary quivers as she watches the girl's fingers manipu-
late that snake of an organ, stroking it and pulling at it
and cajoling it until it stiffens and rises and swells and
trembles under the girl's nose.

Vita squeezes Hilary's hand again.

Hilary keeps her eyes locked on the proceedings in the
adjoining room. Hilary watches as now the girl opens her
mouth to wrap her lips over the knob of the man's

swollen penis.

A short gasp comes out of Hilary's throat. She can't help it. Her legs are weak. She grips Vita's hand to steady herself. She watches the sucking, the slow bobbing of the girl's head, the girl's lips sliding back and forth on the pink stalk, back and forth, back and forth, sucking at his organ, the man smiling, lifting his head a bit to contemplate the ceiling, dropping his eyes again to watch the girl's head, the girl's mouth, the girl's lips as they continue moving.

A muttering now and the pace quickens and suddenly the man in the other room is vibrating and shuddering, the girl's hand now pumping at the organ in her mouth, no longer moving her head, her fingers squeezing his penis and pulling at it as the man opens his mouth and rolls his eyes in the moment of his deliverance. The girl holds her head quite still as she takes his sperm. She has the fingers of her right hand curled around the shaft of his organ, but her left hand is relaxed as it rests on her left thigh.

The man gives a final shudder as he withdraws his penis from the girl's mouth.

The girl rises. She turns and she walks to a corner to find a basin that sits on a small stand. With her back towards the man and towards Vita and Hilary, the girl bends her swan-like neck over the basin, her head no longer visible, nothing seen but her slender shoulders and narrow blue dress and the accordion-pleated skirt that flares out at her knees and sways gently from side to side as she moves her body in front of the basin and the small stand upon which it sits.

—Dear God, Hilary says.

In a whisper. She closes her eyes as she speaks in a whisper.

* * *

On the Boulevard Italiens, Vita is laughing.
—Hilary, darling. . .
—That was too much.
—Haven't you ever?
—Certainly not.
—It's not that horrible, you know. It can be rather nice.
—It's disgusting.
—Not really.
—That girl is a whore, isn't she?
Vita laughs again.
—Yes, of course she is.
—How awful.
They stroll along the boulevard. They stop occasionally
to glance at a shop window. Hilary is quivering again as
she remembers the scene in that room, the man standing,
the girl seated on the velvet-covered bench. What a
world, Hilary thinks. Here we are strolling on the
boulevard. Hilary shudders again. Her breasts are tight.
She avoids the eyes of the pedestrians as she suddenly
imagines they can see into the dark places in her mind.
Or maybe it's Vita who does the seeing now. Vita smiles
at Hilary again as she takes Hilary's hand and leads her
on. Hilary wants to pull her hand away but Vita's grasp is
too firm. Hilary never likes to be touched in public. Now
she has the images again, the girl's mouth sliding on the
length of the man's penis. Well, it's not the first time, is
it? She saw the same when she spied on Walter and the
maid in that hotel. But not the same because she didn't
see as much. Not as clearly as this time. How awful to
have that brutish thing in one's mouth. She can't imagine
Vita doing that. Or maybe she can imagine it. Vita finally
allows Hilary the freedom of her hand. Vita stops at
another shop window and she points at a clever green hat.
—I think I fancy that.
—Please, Vita, not now. . .

—All right, I won't.

But they never did anything except the sucking, Hilary
thinks. Are there really men who come to those places
for nothing but that? She won't ask Vita. Hilary quivers
as she thinks of it. She feels a confusion. Vita looks at
Hilary's face and Vita smiles.

—I think you're still upset.

—No, I'm not.

—Excited.

—Vita, please. . .

And Vita laughs again.

* * *

Now they sit at a café table and Vita talks about her
life in Paris and Hilary's life in Paris and Hilary's little
difficulty with Walter. Just a little difficulty, really. But
Hilary wonders if Vita isn't a darling hypocrite. Does she
have her own difficulties with Charles? The waiter brings
the sherbet and Vita smiles again as she talks about
Walter. Hilary hears only half of it. She tastes the sherbet, rolls the cold sweetness over her tongue. No matter
what you pretend, you can't pretend forever, Hilary. Vita
is talking. Hilary gazes at Vita's arms, at the smooth pink
flesh of Vita's arms. This is Paris, darling. Hilary has a
sudden image of Vita in the nude. How stupid, really.
She's probably as thin as a rail. All these amusements in
Paris. That awful establishment and that horrible woman
Madame Mathilde. Hilary, you need to face your convic-
tions. Vita seems to love Paris so much. She seems to
enjoy things. The amusements. The sexual amusements,
darling. Well, she'd been there before, hadn't she? This
wasn't Vita's first visit to that bordello. Hilary wonders
about the other occasions. She imagines Vita welcomed
by Madame Mathilde. Think about it, Hilary. Then she
thinks of the maid again, the bitch Therese. Yes, darling,

you're obliged to pretend. Walter is such a fool. In the beginning she thought he was such a dashing figure. I want revenge. I'm not at all grateful to him.

—Hilary?

—Yes?

—You need to enjoy Paris, Hilary. Be adventurous, darling. It's really a great cure, you know. You must be adventurous.

* * *

This is a schoolyard in the year 1914. We see Hilary and two other girls. Hilary is in the foreground, facing the other two girls, her back to us, her arms raised and in her two hands a netball.

Between Hilary and the two girls is a pole fixed in the ground, a pole that supports the ring and the white net.

In the background is the wall of the schoolyard and an open gate.

A game of netball.

All three girls wear dark dresses and dark cotton stockings. Hilary wears white shoes. The other girls wear black shoes.

The two girls on the other side of the pole stand with their hands at their sides as they watch Hilary.

Hilary holds the ball with two hands. She moves forward, tilts her body with her eyes on the net.

—Hilary, you always take so long!

Hilary slowly tosses the ball in a high arc.

4.

—Well, it's good, Jack says. The soup is a bit of the all right.

Hilary winces at the bit of the all right. She hates it when he talks like that, the awful talk of Jack and Walter and all the others. She sits across the table from Jack in this little restaurant, sitting here so aware of Jack's eyes on her. Does he think she's pretty? Well, it doesn't matter now, does it? She's here with him now at their secret rendezvous. How clever of him to arrange the lunch in the restaurant of this hotel. Not an ugly place, really. The lobby reminds her of an enormous salon. She wears a white dress, and now for the first time it occurs to her that in actuality it's a virginal white.

Hilary, you're still afraid, aren't you?

Yes, she is. She feels the uneasiness, the fear of discovery. She feels the tightness in her bosom. She wonders if any of the other diners have seen her somewhere. What a messy life she has now. She could never imagine doing this with Jack. What it proves is that her imagination has always been limited. Here she sits at a rendezvous with Walter's friend Jack and Jack is so damned enthusiastic about it. All that enthusiasm shining out of his face, out of his dancing eyes and his pink cheeks. Dear God, what a mess, Hilary thinks. She wanted it and now she has it. She has Jack and the soup that's a bit of the all right and she has the beginning of her revenge against Walter. You poor little girl, Hilary thinks. You poor little girl. You're going up to that room with him and commit adultery with him, aren't you, darling? What an awful time it will be. She can't imagine herself doing it now. How can she possibly imagine it?

Jack's radiance remains undiminished.

—You're making me extremely happy, Hilary.

—Well, good.

—You know how much I care for you.

Is it a necessity for him to say that? Hilary glances out the large window behind Jack, at the shadow of the tree in the garden. She's bored with Jack, bored with his

radiant face and his pink hands. She decides that what he
needs is a metamorphosis of some kind. She decides he
ought to be a soldier, go off to war and march at the front
somewhere. They all talk about the war, but none of
them were in it. They all talk about it and whenever they
do talk about it, Hilary hates it. She hates it when they
talk about Harvard and she hates it when they talk about
the war. But still Jack ought to wear a uniform of some
kind. He'd be a bit more appealing in a uniform.

—You ought to be married, Hilary says.

Jack stares at her.

—Really?

—You ought to find an American girl and marry her.

—I'm only thirty.

—Walter is thirty.

—Well, I'm not Walter, am I?

—Don't you have any girls? American girls?

Jack smiles.

—Yes, a few.

—And you sleep with them, I suppose.

He shows an expression of astonishment now. And
then the expression vanishes to be replaced by an expression of amusement again. Hilary hates the way he snickers at her. She hates the way the sunlight is now striking
the left side of his forehead. He's a Harvard man, all
right. Walter's chum. Walter's pal. Yes, she wants to
sleep with him but it's not at all what he thinks it is. He
thinks he knows the reason, but of course he doesn't and
of course it's better that he doesn't. Hide your eyes,
Hilary thinks. Don't let him read your eyes. He mustn't
see that he means nothing to you. You don't want him to
see that.

—Tell me about your women.

—My women?

—Your women, Jack. You haven't been an angel here
in Paris. You're not an angel, are you?

When they leave the restaurant, she takes his arm, slips
a hand into the crook of his arm as though she and Jack
are man and wife or ancient lovers now strolling so casually from the hotel restaurant through the enormous lobby
to the wide staircase covered with red carpeting.

Hilary is thankful that no one is paying them the slight-
est bit of attention. Jack is still chattering about something, patting her hand, bubbling with a great deal of happiness as they slowly ascend the carpeted stairs.

—We're on the first floor. I had to shout at them to get
something overlooking the garden.

She feels no intimacy. She tells herself she ought to
feel an intimacy of some kind before they actually do
anything. You ought to feel something, Hilary. You
really ought to feel something.

The room is more pleasant than she expects, a large
room with two enormous windows looking out on the
garden and beyond that a corner of the Louvre. They
stand here in the room like two strangers, and then Jack
walks over to one of the windows and he opens it as he
talks about the hotel again.

—You do like it, don't you?

—Yes.

He shows his enthusiasm again. Hilary turns away a
moment to hide any sign of disturbance in her face. Then
someone knocks on the door and the champagne arrives
on a rolling cart pushed by a uniformed porter. Hilary
avoids the porter's eyes and in a moment the porter is
gone and the door is closed and bolted and now she's
alone with Jack again.

The end of the play, Hilary thinks. No, it's not the end,
it's merely the beginning. She looks at the open window,
at the lovely garden, at the large elm tree that reminds
her so much of home.

—Lovely weather, Jack says.

He opens the champagne, laughing as he fills Hilary's

glass, laughing again as he fills his own glass and then
raises it to offer a toast to Hilary.

—To the prettiest girl in Paris.

* * *

Is this Pawtucket? No, this is not Pawtucket; this is a
bench on the boardwalk in Providence.

Hilary sits with a girlfriend and a young man. The
girlfriend sits between Hilary and the young man and the
girlfriend is smiling. Hilary and the young man are looking at each other, but the girlfriend seems to ignore them
as she looks at the sea and smiles.

Hilary wears a white boater hat with a blue headband
and a long white dress. The young man wears a white cap
and he sits with his legs crossed and his right arm resting
on the bench and folded so that his right hand touches his
mouth.

Hilary's friend wears a flowered hat and she holds a
closed parasol along the length of her dark skirt.

Hilary and the young man continue looking at each
other.

Hilary's girlfriend continues smiling at the sea.

—Well, we ought to get back, shouldn't we?

The young man moves his hand against his mouth.

—Tell me your names.

Hilary's friend giggles.

—I won't do that.

The young man looks at Hilary again.

—And you?

Hilary smiles and she turns her face away.

—You don't need to know, do you? And if you do
want to know, I won't tell you.

* * *

Jack has his arm around Hilary's waist.

Hilary wonders if it's a punishment, some unexpected attempt by God to punish her. She remains motionless as Jack's face moves in, as his lips touch her lips, as he kisses her and squeezes her waist with his hand. It's a judgment, Hilary thinks. I'm being judged. I wanted Walter to be judged but now it's me that's being judged.

And now she's in Jack's arms. She does her best not to move, not to make a sound as he kisses her. Only silence is safe. There is safety only in complete silence. Another kiss. He kisses her again. She keeps her lips tightly closed. She holds her tongue captive in her mouth. Jack presses against her as he kisses her. Then his hands slide over her back and down to her buttocks. He squeezes the rounds of her buttocks through her white dress. It's the first intimate touch, the first time he's touched her like that. A shudder runs through Hilary's body as she realizes how afraid she is. What an awful thing it is to be afraid. She has her mind on her fear and suddenly she's aware that Jack has forced her lips apart, pushed her lips apart with his tongue and now his tongue is sliding between her teeth, his tongue sliding over her tongue, his tongue so thick and wet in her open mouth, his hands clutching at her buttocks and his tongue pushing inside her mouth and his breathing heavy against her face.

He needs it, Hilary thinks. He needs to satisfy his pride. She quivers again as Jack slides his right hand between their bodies and upwards to squeeze her right breast through her dress. He fondles her, his left hand fondling her buttocks and his right hand fondling her breasts. He holds the masses of her flesh in his hands as he works his tongue in her mouth.

Hilary thinks about her revenge. She thinks about all those conversations with Walter in the early days of their marriage. She thinks of the questions, all the questioning they did of each other. She thinks of the days of love. Am I an icy-hearted woman? We did make promises, didn't we? We did make the promises. Yes, she does want revenge. He's a bloody bastard and she does want revenge. And now it's here; now she's here offering herself to Walter's chum Jack. Now she has Jack's feverish hands on her body. He's pinching her nipple now. He's found her nipple and he's pinching it and it's not something she likes at all. She hates the way he grips her, the way his hand grips her bottom. She does her best not to move or make a sound or do anything to make matters any worse for her. Dear God, it's awful enough as it is. How can I? Hilary, darling, how can you? Well, you need to think of revenge, don't you? You need to think of revenge if it's to go any further than this.

Than a shudder passes through her again as she feels the poking at her belly, the push of Jack's organ at the front of her body.

You're not stopping it now, Hilary. Is the window still open? What a wild thing it is to be in this room with a man who's not her husband. And Jack Wilson of all people. She's never thought of him as having anything down there. Sometimes she notices a man and she can't think of anything else, but it's never been like that with Jack. Yes, he does have something down there, doesn't he? He has a randy stalk down there and I can feel it. Go on, touch it, Hilary. You're a grown woman and you haven't come here with Jack for anything else. You haven't, darling; you just haven't.

She touches him. Just her fingertips sliding over the front of his trousers. She hears the noise of the street floating in through the open window from beyond the garden. She feels no modesty now. She doesn't care what Jack thinks. She doesn't care whether or not Jack is surprised that she's touching him. She finds the bulge, the hardness, the extent of his erection and she squeezes it with her fingers.

Hilary has a sudden memory of her mother. What a

lark. What a stupid thing to think of her mother at a time like this. Jack mumbles something in Hilary's ear, a sound of desperation in his throat as his fingers work to unbutton the front of his trousers.

—Hilary, darling. . .

He fumbles in his trousers and then finally he exposes his organ. Hilary looks down at it, her eyes on the swollen pink flesh, on the rod that throbs now with the beating of Jack's heart. Yes, he has a certain pride in it. She looks at it. She has a crazy thought that it's really Walter's penis and not Jack's. She curls her fingers around the stem and she squeezes it as if to make certain it's really Jack in this room and not Walter.

Hilary adores his eagerness. Yes she does. Poor Jack is so eager for it. What a great victory it is for him. She's Walter's wife and this is the hand of Walter's wife on Jack's tumescent manhood. Jack's head is bent as he looks down to watch her hand, her fingers, the curling of her fingers around his penis. His eyes are feverish. What a simple creature he is. Hilary squeezes his penis again. Then she laughs and she pulls away from him.

—We really ought to undress. Don't you think so, Jack? We really ought to get our clothes off.

Jack nods, his penis jerking as it soars out of the opening in his trousers. Then he looks away and he begins the removal of his clothes. He mutters something but his voice is too indistinct. Hilary watches him as she unbuttons her dress. She wants to laugh but she clenches her teeth and she stops it. She looks at the open window, at the trees in the garden, at the corner of the Louvre and the blue sky above it. You must pretend, Hilary thinks. This is a world filled with pretending and you must pretend like the others. She unsnaps her brassiere and she doesn't mind Jack staring at her. She faces him now without any hesitation. Go on, look Hilary thinks. She doesn't mind that he stares at her nipples. Well, damn it,

I have breasts, don't I? Hilary pulls at the waistband of her lace-edged silk knickers. She pulls at the pink silk with her eyes on the open window as she finishes undressing herself. It's done now. It's a bright afternoon and she's naked in a room with Jack Wilson. Is Walter feeling it? Is Walter feeling a twinge in his belly without knowing why? Hilary quivers. Oh damn Walter. Oh damn Walter and Jack. Oh damn them all, all of them, every damn one of them.

Then Hilary gasps as she suddenly feels Jack's hand on her body. He kisses her. He kisses her breasts, her nipples. He mumbles against her skin as he squeezes her waist. Hilary shudders as she feels his hands on her buttocks. She tilts her head to the side to have a look at his penis. It's like a snake, really, an awful serpent with a tiny mouth and no eyes at all. Her nipples are wet as Jack licks at them. Then he pushes her towards the bed and she suddenly finds herself down on the mattress on her back. She wonders what he has in his mind as she lies there with her legs dangling over the side of the bed. They do what they want, she thinks. They always do what they want.

Jack kneels on the carpet. Hilary groans when she sees it. Darling, you're afraid, aren't you? Her legs tremble as he touches and strokes them and raises them to his shoulders. Darling, you're afraid. And now he's kissing her knees, her thighs, the insides of her thighs and finally her centerpiece. Jack's mouth is on her quim. His mouth is on her sex. Dear God, he's sniffing at it. She hears a whimpering sound and she suddenly realizes it's her own voice, her own throat that's whimpering. He has her sex in his mouth, her female flesh in his mouth, his hands stroking her thighs as he draws the pleasure out of her throat. She cranes her neck to look down at him, but all she can see is the top of his head and his closed eyes and his nose pushing at the curls of her little garden.

Oh Hilary, you do adore it, don't you? She tosses her
head back and she closes her eyes to savor it. It's like
having an animal sucking at her quim, a hungry little
animal with a warm wet tongue so avid and so restless.
Dear God, I'm impressed, Hilary thinks. It's Jack Wilson
after all and she didn't expect it. Does he do this to all his
women? She's had it only once before in her life and that
wasn't her husband. Just a boy from Yale with too much
to drink on the lawn of a house in New Haven. Sucking
at her sex like a wild thing while she lay there on the
grass pretending to be too drunk to understand it. Well,
she understands it now. She understands Jack's tongue.
He has his tongue in all her secret places. He has his nose
in the wet, in the wet of her sex. It's really quite different
from the other thing. She can't imagine Walter doing it.
She can't imagine Walter sucking at her like this. She
can't imagine he ever does it to anyone. Not to the maid.
Hilary shudders as she thinks of Walter and the maid. Is
it human nature? Jack is so eager as he does it. Hilary
rocks her legs in the air as she feels his tongue sliding in
and out of her grotto. She has a hole down there and Jack
Wilson has his tongue in it. What a delight. What a
delight to feel it. No, it's awful, isn't it? It's not a delight,
it's awful. The way he sucks at the wet, it's really awful.
I don't want it. It's too much and I really don't want it.
What a stupid little goose he is to suck at it like that. I
don't want it, you fool, I don't want it.

Then at last Jack pulls away, his mouth wet, his eyes
burning. Hilary feels nothing now. She looks at him once
and then she turns her head to avoid his eyes. Just the
two of us, she thinks. And she quivers as he climbs onto
the bed and hovers over her. He pulls at her legs and
raises them and mounts her. Mounting her. She hears a
noise in the garden, a crackling sound. Or is it the street
beyond? Hilary feels Jack's organ, his penis pushing at
her sex. She suddenly thinks of herself as a harem girl, a

concubine to some Oriental potentate, a houri living in
Oriental splendor and now mounted by her king. His
organ pushes in. She's a woman after all and she feels it.
She feels the stretching, the pushing of his throbbing
flesh. Jack groans as he lurches forward. He's not like
Walter. He's more adept than Walter. He pushes at her
again and he makes a sound in his throat. Do you like it,
Hilary? Do you fancy his organ in there? I have a craving
for life, she thinks. She steals a glance at Jack's face, at
his clenched jaws and his flushed cheeks. This is one of
the mysteries, isn't it? She holds his arms with her hands.
She thinks of the garden outside the window. This is
Paris, isn't it? And now a shudder passes through her as
she feels Jack's balls slapping against her buttocks. She
hasn't touched him at all, just that bit of fondling before
he pushed her onto the bed. She wonders what sort of
boy he was. Does he still have a house somewhere? Dear
God, the way he pushes at her. Does he find her receptive? In the beginning Walter liked to whisper how receptive she was. It's womanly, isn't it? How receptive are
the Blairs of Boston? They don't like her, do they? Well,
Jack seems to like her. Jack has the fire in his eyes and
he does seem to like her. Don't make any predictions,
Hilary. You know when you make predictions they never
seem to come true. He's pounding her now, his organ
pounding her poor little thing, his penis pounding her sex
as he breathes at her ear. No expectations, Hilary. Please,
darling, no expectations.

Jack is pumping now, his hips churning as he continues
pumping in Hilary's wet sex. What an effort, Hilary
thinks. He's not like Walter. The tempo is so different.
Jack lunges at the end of each stroke and she feels completely penetrated by him. Once again she feels his balls
slapping at her buttocks. His knackers. I'm a girl and I
don't have knackers in my knickers, thank you. Nothing
but despair, Hilary. He keeps his penis sliding in there.

She suddenly wonders what he thinks of her. What opinion does he have? Dear God, the bed is creaking. I hate it so when the bed creaks. I'm sure they can hear it in the garden. They're having their tea down there and they can hear the bed creaking. Everyone in the world can hear this bed creaking.

Jack grunts. He lurches forward once more as he finishes. Hilary watches the joy in his face, the twisting of his mouth as he grinds against her sex.

Well, it's over, isn't it? Now for the first time she notices the carved molding in the ceiling. Flowers and leaves. She lies there under Jack feeling a bit dull as she stares at the white ceiling.

* * *

—You don't need to feel guilty, Hilary.

—Why not?

—I know you're thinking about loyalty and all that. But there's a spark between us and we just couldn't ignore it.

—Couldn't we?

—Walter won't ever know about this. I promise you I won't ever tell him.

—Does Walter sleep with other women?

—You don't want me to talk about that.

—Yes, I do want you to talk about it. Does he?

—I don't know, actually.

—You're his best friend.

—We don't talk about it. It's just one of those things we don't talk about.

* * *

A laugh; a bubbling laugh. A café near the Gare Saint-Lazare. Marceline sits between two sailors. She has her left arm around the shoulders of the older one, her right hand on the knee of the younger sailor, her head tilted as she smiles at him.

Marceline wears a white sailor blouse and a dark skirt. The blouse is tight and it shows the curves of her breasts.

Marceline nudges the younger sailor with her elbow.

—Should I get another girl?

The sailor shrugs.

—Ask him.

—He's too drunk to know what he wants.

—How come you're not in a house? You're a pretty one for a place like this.

Marceline pouts.

—I don't like a house that much. The men are too old and I don't like it.

5.

Here are the tall trees on the road to Versailles, each tree like a tall sentinel against the clear blue sky, each tree with its arms raised in a silent oblation.

Walter laughs as he drives the motorcar.

The warm breeze blows at the brim of Hilary's hat, at the sleeve of her dress as she holds the hat with her raised hand.

—What a damn nice car, Walter says.

It's a Voisin, a big car borrowed from a friend. Walter says he intends to buy one and he intends to have a new chauffeur. Walter likes the power of the car. Hilary closes her eyes as Walter continues shouting at her about the motor of the motorcar, the motor and the wheels and the motor again and now the headlamps and the windows. Hilary decides that Walter might drive the Voisin into another car at this speed and they'll all be killed outright. It's a good car, all right. As nearly as possible, it's a good

car, but they'll all be killed anyway. The trees move by
so fast she can hardly count them. She's frightened; she's
more than a little frightened. She's thankful the road is so
straight. This is such a straight road through the trees to
Versailles, such a straight road past Sevres. Like Mother,
Hilary thinks. I'm sitting here so much like Mother, a
married woman seated beside her husband in a motorcar.
Now Hilary turns her face up to get more of the sun on
her cheeks. She tells herself she does not want to be like
her mother. There's not much of a resemblance, is there?
    Walter laughs.
    —You like it, don't you?
    —Yes.
    He laughs again. He's like a man with a sudden revela-
tion. He holds the wheel of the Voisin and he laughs as
he has his sudden revelation. People on the road are staring at them. The heads are turning as they pass.
    —What a damn nice car, Walter says.

                    *   *   *

    A grand piano? Yes they had a grand piano in the
house in Pawtucket. Hilary's father is here seated on the
piano stool. He wears a white shirt, a grey tweed suit,
white shoes. Both hands are on the keys, his face turned
to the left, perhaps to look at someone, perhaps in a pose
of musical authenticity. Behind his right shoulder and at
the edge of the piano stands Hilary's mother.
    This is the year 1912 and Hilary's mother wears a long
white skirt that covers her ankles, a white high-necked
blouse with long sleeves. She has her hair put up in a
bun, her head tilted forward, her eyes on the music sheet
that sits on the piano in front of her husband.
    Now Hilary's father turns his face further to the left. Is
he looking at Hilary? Then he turns to the right to look at
his wife.

—It's a bit warm, isn't it?

Hilary's mother nods.

—Yes, I think so.

—We need the windows open, don't we? We need some fresh air.

—I'll tell the servants.

—And tell Bessie to bring me some tea, will you? I'm not going to play anything without my tea.

* * *

On a Wednesday afternoon Hilary walks in the Luxembourg gardens. She does enjoy the Luxembourg. She walks alone along the gravel path. For the moment she has an interlude of peace. She gazes at the trees as she passes them. She tells herself that after all life isn't that bad; it's not that bad after all. She needs to face her difficulties; she needs to be face to face with things.

When they first came to Paris, she often walked with Walter in these gardens. Hilary wonders now if she ought to tell Walter everything. Or tell him almost everything. She can't tell it all, can she?

Hilary passes an old woman sitting on a bench and she avoids the old woman's eyes.

I don't want to be like that, Hilary thinks. Then she tells herself she's really no better than the old woman and it's silly of her to be petulant. And so now Hilary wonders if the old woman likes her dress. She wonders if the old woman is amused. She wonders what sort of amusement an old woman like that has.

The air is so clean in the Luxembourg.

You must take precautions, Hilary thinks.

She hears a child laugh. Then another child. Two children are playing in a small enclosure set aside for them. How lovely it is to see children playing like that in the Luxembourg. Hilary thinks of Walter again as she passes another old woman seated on a bench. How ridiculous I am, Hilary thinks. What a mess I've made of my marriage. She looks at the trees again. She wants to cry now, but she hates the thought of dealing with her tears.

Then she feels a twinge of guilt again. How awful of me to deceive Walter with one of his friends. If it's true that Walter pokes the maid, it's also true that maids don't count. They don't, do they? Men like Walter need their pleasures. It's only a maid in Paris, a little twit of a girl with a big arse. Men are so much like hungry dogs. One little sniff and they lose their senses. Hilary remembers with pleasure now the way Jack sniffed at her sex. She gazes at the blue sky again. She hears the laughter of a child somewhere. Why think of all the cruel things in life? It's only a maid, isn't it? What a lovely place this is. Hilary quivers as a smell of flowers comes to her nose. She remembers now that Walter once remarked that his father was fond of stroking the maids on occasion. The son does the same as the father.

I don't like adultery, Hilary thinks. She's annoyed at the crunching sound of the gravel beneath her feet. A shudder passes through her as she remembers the way Jack smiled at her. Is Jack still smiling? Hilary exits the Luxembourg still entangled in her uncertainties. She tugs at her cloche hat as she finds herself standing alone in the Boulevard St. Michel.

* * *

At a café table Hilary sits with a coffee and a small ugly-looking cake and her eyes on the poules across the road. Three girls stand in a Montparnasse alcove offering themselves to each man that passes. Hilary is surprised at how young the girls are. She always thinks of the whores as old wrecks; but these girls are young and not wrecks at all. One of them, at least, seems quite beautiful.

Life is so short, Hilary thinks. She glances now at the
other patrons of the café. She wonders what they think of
her. What torture it is to be so uncertain of things. The
waiter hurries by with his red nose in the air. Hilary
turns her head slowly to stare at the poules again. An old
man passes on the sidewalk with a look of stupefaction on
his face. The street is hardly busy now. It's a dull afternoon, an ordinary dull afternoon that promises nothing.
She wishes she could hear the sound of her own voice.
I'm too alone, she thinks. She gazes at the poules again.
Each time a man passes them, they seem about to grasp
him, capture him in their arms and hold him.

Then, at last, a man stops and one of the poules has her
customer. They talk a bit and then they walk off together.
Hilary is surprised because the girl isn't the prettier one.
She doesn't understand it.

More charming, Hilary thinks. Well, don't think about
it. You don't want to be obsessed about something like
that.

—Hilary, darling. . .

A voice, a pair of dazzled eyes. It's Arthur Compton,
Walter's chum Arthur strolling off the sidewalk and
between the tables with his lips in a wide smile under his
brown moustache.

—Hello, Arthur.

—What a lovely treat to find you here. I was just
wondering if I ought to sit down somewhere and rest my
legs.

—You've been walking.

—Yes, I've been walking. I've walked a hundred miles,
I think.

So here he is at her table now with his cheery talk.
Hilary tells herself she wanted someone and now she has
him. Now she can hear the sound of her voice again. She
agrees to have some brandy with Arthur. He's not a bad
sort, really. A bit dull. Much duller than Jack. Or is he?

How much can a woman actually tell about a man? Well,
he looks dull. There's nothing bold about him; even his
coloring is subdued. Are the patrons looking at them?
Hilary decides that maybe Arthur has a poet's soul. She
glances at the poules again. The pretty girl is gone and
only one of the whores remains in the alcove. All for
money, Hilary thinks. She nods and smiles at Arthur's
babbling. He's talking about his tailor now. He says he
wants to go to London to put some decent clothes in his
wardrobe. He says Hilary's hat is the loveliest hat he's
seen in Paris.

A thousand francs, Hilary thinks. It's a thousand-franc
hat and she's pleased that Arthur likes it. She lifts her
brandy and she sips it and she smiles at Arthur again.

Arthur's eyes continue to fly over Hilary's face as he
talks to her. Hilary wonders about his life here in Paris.
He works in a bank somewhere. Walter says that Arthur
has all the money he needs. Oh, he's flirting with me,
Hilary thinks. She's quite certain that Arthur is flirting
with her. Maybe he thinks it's the thing to do here. Or
maybe it's more than that and he's after Walter's wife.
Hilary tries to imagine herself with Arthur Compton.
Debauched, Hilary thinks. It's a question of debauchery,
isn't it? He can't possibly know about her and Jack. That
would be awful, wouldn't it? Now she's aware of the eyes
of the patrons again. These Frenchmen are so knowing
about things. Hilary wonders again what they think of
her. What sort of woman do they think she is? She
quivers at the excitement in Arthur's eyes. He's talking
about the beauty of some of the statues in the Louvre.
Well, I don't give a damn about the statues in the Louvre,
Hilary thinks. She turns her eyes away as the waiter
arrives. I don't give a damn about the statues in the
Louvre. Walter is always talking about those statues and
I don't give a damn about either Walter or the Louvre or
the damn statues in the Louvre or the fat white arse of

my cheap little maid.

Arthur smiles at Hilary.

—You're a lovely girl, you know. Walter's a damn lucky fellow.

* * *

This isn't much of a room, but it does have a small sofa. Still dressed, Hilary and Arthur occupy the sofa in the midst of a frenzied kiss. Hilary leans against Arthur's left shoulder with her face turned up to get his moustached lips pressed upon her mouth. Arthur has his left arm curled around Hilary's shoulders and his left hand curving down to enclose the slope of Hilary's left breast. Hilary's dress is pulled back along her thighs, her left thigh exposed almost to the buttock, the lower part of her thigh covered by Arthur's right hand. Hilary's right arm and right hand cannot be seen. She has her left hand closed around Arthur's penis, her fingers clutching it through his trousers, four fingers curled tightly around the shaft and her thumb pressed against the outline of his knob.

Arthur's mouth is wet and his moustache tickles Hilary's lips.

Well, it's not splendor, Hilary thinks. It's not a splendorous thing, is it? She hates this ugly little hotel room. Someone is shrieking with happiness in the courtyard. Or is it someone awakening from a midday nightmare? Arthur's hands aren't moving much. He holds her thigh as if he doubts its existence and he holds her breast as if he's fearful it might vanish. Now he squeezes her breast, his fingers squeezing her flesh through her clothes. Does he like the boyish line? He's not like Jack or Walter. Jack made such an amusing fuss over her breasts. Arthur is a man who likes a bit of feminine daintiness. He's kissing her neck now, his moustache tickling the slope of her neck, his breath warm against her skin as his hands continue to clutch at her body. They all like a pretty woman, don't they? He wants her body. He wants her breasts and her legs and what she has between her legs.

Hilary opens one eye to look at the sheen of sweat on Arthur's temples.

She hears the sound of an accordion. Somewhere outside the window someone is playing an accordion.

—Let me undress you, Arthur says.

—All right.

She stands up. She stands quietly as his hands fumble with her clothes. She looks down at his brown hair and she tells herself that he's not at all her type of man. Well, neither is Jack then. Nor even Walter, for that matter. Arthur seems to be whispering something. Hilary decides the room is stifling hot and more horrible than she expected. Arthur's fingers work at the buttons and hooks and finally he has her dress sliding down her thighs. Success in his eyes as her dress slides down. She imagines she can hear his heart pounding. Oh, you're silly, Hilary thinks. The accordion is playing again, the music rising and falling and rising again. Hilary has a sudden feeling she's on a stage somewhere, on the stage of a theater, standing there on a stage while Arthur Compton removes her clothes piece by piece. He's kissing her again. Now he's kissing her thighs above the tops of her stockings. He ought to be a servant. She decides Arthur would make a proper butler. Does he want her on the bed now? He's mumbling again as he runs his hands over the globes of her buttocks. Why not? Hilary thinks. She doesn't care anymore. She doesn't care about his mumbling. She doesn't mind the way he stares at her little bush. He almost has his nose in it. Hilary bumps her pelvis forward and then he does have his nose in it. She wants to giggle but she restrains it. Well, go on, Arthur. He slips to his knees now. He's gurgling at her, his nose in her

bush and his tongue fluttering between the lips of her
bijou. He wants her treasure. Arthur Compton is a pirate
and he wants her treasure. She's Walter's wife and Arthur
Compton has her knickers off and he wants her treasure.
What a luxury it is to have his tongue in there. He makes
noises as he does it. Hilary spreads her thighs for him.
She keeps her head bent and her thighs apart as Arthur
mumbles at her sex. The way he's kneeling on the carpet
with his head up, she could sit on his face if she wanted
it. No, she doesn't want it. She's in the throes now. She
moans at him as she humps her bush at his mouth. She
tells herself he's much better than Jack. Yes, Arthur has
more initiative. Arthur shows more industry. He's kissing
her thighs now. He runs his mouth up and down the skin
of her thighs. His mouth is wet and his moustache tickles
her. Hilary moans as she has a sudden convulsion. Arthur
returns his tongue to her sex and now he's much more
forceful. She touches his head. She fondles his head with
her hands as he sucks at her sex. She keeps her head
bent. She stares at the top of Arthur Compton's head. She
keeps her eyes on the top of Arthur's head as she rolls
her hips in a trembling dance.

* * *

Arthur's mouth is wet.
—You're giving me a great joy, Hilary.
—You ought to get your clothes off, don't you think?
—Yes, of course I will. It's marvelous, isn't it? We're
like two souls that have found each other. I never imagined it, you know. I never imagined it would be possible.

Hilary is astonished when she discovers his masculine
attributes are formidable indeed. Much larger than she
expected. All that clutching through his trousers had
revealed nothing to her. She hasn't enough experience to

know a man by the feel of him. But now she has him in
front of her eyes and the large organ curving over a pair
of massive testicles has her befuddled. There's more of
the animal in Arthur Compton than she ever suspected.

—You're big.

Arthur laughs.

—Most women like it.

His eyes are on her body. They know about each other
now. He's had his tongue in her sex and now she has the
measure of him. He takes Hilary's hands and he makes
her rise and he kisses her again. She feels that great
boom of a penis pushing against her belly. Arthur makes
her turn. He wants her on the bed. He wants her kneeling
on the bed. Hilary quivers as she does what he wants.
She hears him mumbling at her as she kneels on the bed.
She feels his hands on her buttocks. She drops her head
slowly as she moves her knees apart. She's a bit shocked
by what she's doing. Arthur is completely delighted with
her. Well, all right, Hilary thinks. She doesn't mind his
hands on her buttocks. She doesn't mind that he's looking
at her that way. She tells herself she doesn't care one way
or the other. The animals do it this way and even if she's
never had it this way she doesn't mind trying it. She
doesn't mind one way or the other and she doesn't mind
trying it.

—Lovely, Arthur says.

All she wants now is the end of it.

Arthur groans as he pushes his organ inside. Hilary
keeps her eyes closed. She has a sudden feeling that
Arthur is stealing something from her. He's pilfering
something. She feels his huge penis in her sex and she
tells herself she doesn't like it. She hates the way he
strokes her buttocks. Oh, she doesn't care. You don't
care, do you, darling? He's mumbling again. He's mumbling sweet phrases as he strokes his organ in and out of
her body. She feels the excitement in his hands, in the

sliding of his penis. Lord, what a frenzy now. He's calling her an angel. He squeezes her buttocks as he calls
her an angel. Hilary's mouth opens as she feels his hands
on her buttocks again. Yes, this is different than that time
with Jack. What a surprise it is. What a surprise Arthur
Compton is. He's almost whimpering now as he strokes
her skin. She keeps her eyes closed. He's like an animal,
isn't he? She hears the music again. She hears the accordion.

Well, it's two, Hilary thinks. They've both had me.
Jack and Arthur. Walter's chums Jack and Arthur. Now
they have more in common than just the years at Harvard. They've both had me. They've both had Walter's
wife and now they have more in common.

The accordion rises and falls and rises again.

Hilary reaches back with a hand now. She reaches back
with her right hand to find the massive balls under the
sliding organ.

Bigger than Walter, isn't he? Hilary closes her eyes as
she waits for the next rising of the accordion.

* * *

Arthur looks pensive.

—I suppose you think I'm a traitor to Walter.

—Are you?

—I don't know. Yes, I suppose so. But I couldn't help
it, Hilary. I think you've bewitched me.

—Bewitched by a witch.

—You're not a witch.

—Yes, I'm a witch.

—It's my fault, isn't it? Now I'll never forgive myself.

—Poor Arthur.

—It's awful, isn't it?

—Does Walter sleep with other woman?

—I don't know.

—French girls? He likes French girls, doesn't he?
Arthur chuckles.
—We all do, don't we?
—Bordellos, Arthur? Have you gone to a bordello with
Walter?
—Not here in Paris.
—Then where?
—New York. That's before you and Walter were mar-
ried, you understand.
—Yes, I understand.

* * *

A troupe of girls here. Hilary's boarding school is the
Warwick School for Girls, Hastings-on-Hudson, a clump
of ivy-covered buildings in the year 1916, sculptured
hedges, broad lawns, a dozen girls on the gravel path to
one of the buildings, the girls busy talking and laughing,
Hilary holding two books to her chest as she hurries
along in her white dress and black stockings.
—Miss Caldwell is back.
—She's an old witch.
—Oh, there are worse.
—No, there aren't. Caldwell's the one I hate the most.
—Do you hate Caldwell, Hilary?
Hilary lifts her head as she hurries along with them.
—I hate the whole school.
The other girls giggle. The girls in front look back to
see what the giggling is about, and then they look for-
ward again as they enter the door.

6.

•

Henry Meade is an Englishman with an interest in

poetry. He wears a tight white collar and a blue silk cravat. He smiles at Hilary from behind a cluttered desk in a dusty room.

—We're doing four issues a year now, but we'd like to do six. We're quite small, you see.

—I don't mind.

—I can't pay you much.

—I don't care about that either. I just want to keep busy.

—Do you like poetry?

—No, I don't think so.

—Oh dear.

Mr. Meade considers Hilary's employment. He has her sitting in a chair near the door and his eyes continually return to Hilary's legs, her shoes, her silk-covered ankles. He wets his lips. Hilary feels an annoyance. She crosses her legs again. She wishes he wouldn't stare at her ankles like that. She doesn't want that sort of attention. She tells herself that if he becomes at all suggestive, she'll refuse him. She feels a sudden emptiness inside, a complete apathy, a total disinterest now in Henry Meade and his little magazine. She hates the dust on the shelves. I don't care about anyone, Hilary thinks. Yes, it's true. She has no emotional attachments. She finds them all boring. Henry Meade's blue cravat is so boring. The way he stares at her legs is so boring. I don't want it, Hilary thinks; I really don't want it.

—You're a pretty girl, Mr. Meade says.

—I don't like poetry that much.

—Well, it doesn't matter. I do need someone.

—But I don't like poetry that much.

* * *

In the place d'Italie, Marceline is with a man in a café. They have a table in a corner, the mirrored walls behind

them showing the backs of their heads, the gleam of the
man's dark hair, the other patrons, the smoke that hovers
over the other tables.

On the table in front of Marceline is an empty Pernod
glass standing in a white saucer. In front of Marceline's
companion is a teapot in a saucer, a teacup in a saucer,
an open packet of cigarettes.

The man turns his head to look at Marceline.

—You don't want it?

—Darling, I don't want to be shut in somewhere.

—I won't shut you in.

—Oh, yes, you will.

—But you'll have dinner with me tonight, won't you?

She smiles at him and he leans forward to kiss her.
Marceline lifts her lips to his mouth, lifts the cigarette in
her right hand, laughs at him as he touches her breasts
with his fingertips.

* * *

A shadowy alcove now.

Madame Mathilde smiles at Hilary.

—Yes, I remember you. You were here with an
Englishwoman.

—Yes.

Madame Mathilde touches the curls that cover her ears.
She has rose cheeks and red lips and a spot of powder on
her chin. She nods at Hilary. She moves her hand down
to the necklace at her throat, a graceful hand, her shoulders wriggling as she nods at Hilary.

The bench in the alcove is covered with red velvet.
The chairs in the room are in shadows. Hilary thinks she
hears whispering somewhere. People whispering. Dear
God, where are they? Hilary quivers under the eyes of
Madame Mathilde. Hilary wonders what the woman is
thinking.

—Do you want the judas-hole again?
—Is it possible?
—Yes, of course.

Madame Mathilde moves out of the alcove with a rustling of her skirt. Hilary wonders about the women, the girls, the other rooms. She climbs the stairs behind Madame Mathilde, behind the rustling skirt, behind the cloud of perfume, climbing in the quiet of the shadows.

Whispering again. Or am I imagining it? Dear Lord, I don't want them whispering about me.

* * *

It's the same room.

An empty room with shadows. Madame Mathilde smiles at Hilary as she points at the panel that covers the peep-slit.

—In a few moments, I think. You don't mind waiting, do you? Would you like a cigarette?
—No, thank you.

Madame Mathilde leaves, her skirt rustling as she passes through the doorway, the door closing after her, the room silent again.

Hilary moves to the judas-hole and she slides the panel to the right to expose the aperture, the narrow slit. The other room is empty. It's the room as she remembers it, the bed, the draperies, the walls covered with silk.

Suddenly the door opens and a girl and a man enter the room together. Hilary quivers as she watches them. It's a play, Hilary thinks. It's a stage in a theater somewhere. It's not real, is it? The girl is pretty, after all. A girl with dark eyes and bright red lips and white skin. The man is ordinary, well-dressed, middle-aged, his eyes bright as he looks at the girl. He slips his arm around the girl's waist as she kisses his cheek. Then they undress together. They undress together in silence. Hilary feels the beating of her heart as they undress together in silence. The girl's thighs are revealed, her white buttocks, her dark-nippled breasts, the patch of dark fur at the joining of her thighs. The man has pasty white skin and a paunch, his organ limp, his balls dangling out of a forest of dark hair.

The play moves forward, each movement precise, every moment carefully measured, a slow tempo, the pink skin wavering, the shadows trembling.

The girl sits on the edge of the bed as she fondles the weight of the man's testicles. Then the girl rises and she laughs as she leads the man to the basin on the small table against the wall. Hilary quivers with revulsion as she watches the washing of the man's parts. His private parts. His dangling penis and his dangling balls and the girl's slender fingers slowly stroking his flesh until his penis lengthens and thickens and grows into a pink baton.

Is the girl whispering? She leads the man to the bed and she sits on the edge of the mattress again. She's a fine girl, Hilary thinks. She's a polite girl and her politeness is a pleasant thing to watch. Yes, it's pleasant. Oh Hilary, you're a fool, aren't you? Now the girl opens her mouth and Hilary watches carefully as the girl closes her lips over the man's knob. The man shudders. For a moment neither the man nor the girl make any movement at all. The man stands immobile and the girl remains immobile with her lips just covering the bulb of the man's penis and her dark eyes closed.

Hilary stares at the girl's red lips, at the stretching of the girl's red lips.

Now the lips are moving. The girl's mouth is moving, her eyes open again, her lips undulating around the knob of the man's organ.

Is she pretending? Hilary wonders if the girl in the other room is pretending. It's a play, isn't it? It's a stage and the actors are pretending.

Hilary shudders. Her legs are weak. She closes her

eyes and then she opens them again.

The girl is sucking now, her lips moving over the man's organ, her red lips moving, sliding, sucking at his penis. The man's jaw hangs open, his head bent, his eyes on the girl's mouth, his hands now moving to the girl's head.

He holds her head as it moves, his hands holding her head as her head is moving, his hands holding her head as her mouth slides back and forth over his pink organ.

Hilary stands in the dark. Hilary quivers in the dark. She stands with her eyes against the judas-hole, quivering in the dark as the girl's mouth continues the slow sliding, the slow sucking, the movement back and forth on the man's penis.

She holds his balls now. The girl holds the man's testicles as she sucks him, her fingers holding his scrotum, her mouth never ceasing to move as she pulls and fondles his dangling testicles.

Hilary remembers Vita's question: Haven't you ever?

The girl pulls back, pulls her mouth away from the man's penis. A look, a question, a decision. The girl's saliva gleams on his trembling organ. She forms the words with her lips. Hilary hears nothing. She watches them as they move onto the bed, the girl stretching out, the man stretching out, the girl's face blurred now, her face blurred as the man hovers over her.

The girl lies on her back. Her mouth is empty but now her mouth is moving again. She moves her legs, raises her legs, raises her knees. Not a single word is uttered. The man shifts his body and he utters not a single word. Hilary watches the heavy swing of his balls, his penis swaying like a club over the swing of his balls, the girl's knees raised, the broad knob pushing now at the girl's sex, the knob pushing forward into the girl's grotto, the penis encased, the girl turning her head to the side as the penetration is completed.

Her bones, Hilary thinks. The girls appears too fragile
for it. She's a slender girl and Hilary imagines the girl
has delicate bones.

The man is thrusting now, thrusting on the bed, his
buttocks moving in a dance, a waltzing on the bed, his
organ sliding in the girl's wound.

Her quim, Hilary thinks. Hilary wants to touch herself,
touch her own quim as she watches them. Walter has
never once called it by that name. Not by any name,
really. It's an unmentionable thing, isn't it? Hilary wants
to touch herself, but she resists the impulse. She keeps
her eyes at the judas-hole and she resists the impulse.

The man on the bed suddenly pulls his penis out of the
girl's body and he leans back. He mumbles something at
the girl. Hilary strains to hear it, but she can't make it
out. The girl smiles under the man's eyes. The girl rolls
over on her belly, on her knees, raising herself on her
knees, her rump under the man's eyes, the smooth white
skin of her buttocks under the man's drooping jaw.

The girl's head is now turned to face Hilary and the
girl's eyes are closed. Is she asleep? She's not asleep,
Hilary thinks. Hilary watches the slow weaving of the
girl's hips as the man caresses the girl's buttocks. The
man's paunch touches the girl's buttocks as he fingers her
sex. Hilary watches the play of his fingers.

It's not a dream, Hilary thinks. She feels a tightness in
her breasts. She looks at the girl's breasts, at the girl's
dark-nippled breasts that hang now to touch the counterpane.

It's an acceptance, Hilary thinks. It's a question of
abnegation. She remembers Arthur Compton behind her,
his belly pressed against her buttocks, his balls pressed
against her sex.

The man on the bed is at the girl again, one hand holding her hip as the other hand steers his penis into the
girl's channel.

They ought to have music, really. They ought to have a church organ, Hilary thinks. He's poking her now. He has himself deep in her quim and he's poking her. Hilary trembles as she repeats the words in her mind. He's poking her, isn't he? He's poking her. He's poking that girl with his thing in her quim.

He stops.

A shudder passes through the man as he pulls his organ out of the girl's body. His penis dangles turgid and wet as he mumbles again to the girl. The girl replies, but once again Hilary can't make it out. Hilary suddenly thinks of the flowers in the Luxembourg. She watches as the man strokes his penis and lifts it to place his knob against the dark ring of the girl's anus.

I can't bear it, Hilary thinks; oh, I can't bear it.

She hears a sound and she glances at the door a moment. Then her eyes are drawn once again to the judas-hole, the peep-slit, the man's knob now pushing at the girl's anus, pushing and slowly entering, pushing forward as the girl's mouth hangs open, her eyes wide open with a look of surprise.

Pushing in.

Well, he's waking her up, Hilary thinks. That should wake her up, shouldn't it?

The girl shudders. The girl seems transported. The man is moving again, thrusting again, his organ now a solid presence in the girl's rear passage, the girl moving her lips as the man moves, her eyes rolling, her face with a constant expression of surprise.

One last thrust. He finishes. Hilary watches the finishing with her face pressed against the wall. Hilary presses her face against the wall and she's aware of the sweat beneath her eyes. Her legs tremble as she feels the sweat beneath her eyes.

—She's a pretty girl, isn't she?

It's Madame Mathilde, smiling at Hilary, her dark eyes

amused. She tilts her head a bit as she repeats the question.

—She's a pretty girl, isn't she?

—Yes.

—Do you want her? Would you like her to make love to you?

—Oh, no.

—A boy then? Would you like a boy?

Hilary feels a sudden weakness. She tells herself she can't deal with it. She closes her eyes and she trembles as Madame Mathilde repeats the question.

—Would you like a boy?

—I don't know. . .

—Come with me, my dear.

She leads Hilary along, out of the room and down the dark corridor to another room. Madame Mathilde whispers instructions to a maid and in a few moments a young man appears, a boy of twenty, his eyes bright, his body quick with energy.

—This is Julien. As you will see, he can be quite charming.

Madame Mathilde leaves them. Hilary remains alone with the boy, with Julien, with the dark-haired young man who is now smiling at her.

—Madame?

Yes, madame. Hilary feels a madness inside her. Why not? she thinks. Oh dear God, why not? She leans forward and she kisses him. She kisses him again and she fondles him. He's been bought, hasn't he? She runs her fingers over the front of his trousers, over the bulge of his attributes. Yes, why not? The boy has such knowing eyes. He smiles at Hilary as they undress. Hilary finds herself blushing. Is she indeed blushing? She feels so open to the boy. She takes his hand and she kisses him and then she moves to the bed and she kneels upon it. She kneels upon the edge of the bed with her head down

and her rump in the air. The boy says nothing. Hilary
hears her heart beating in the silence. She keeps her eyes
closed. The boy touches Hilary and Hilary shudders.
She's no longer aware of anything but the touch of the
boy's fingers on her buttocks. Then she reaches back to
find his penis and she guides his organ into the grip of
her sex.

In my quim, Hilary thinks. She wonders what his
mother is like. Hilary groans as the boy begins moving
his organ in her body. She closes her eyes again as the
boy drives his penis in and out of her wet sex. Is he still
in school? Hilary reaches back again to touch him, to fondle his balls, blushing as she fondles his balls, blushing as
he pumps his penis. The lamp is lit and she wonders if he
sees her blushing. She feels his thrusting and she wonders
what he feels when he does it. Yes, I want it, Hilary
thinks. She wants his juices in her body. A cry escapes
her throat as the boy finishes, as the boy clutches at her
hips and groans in his pleasure.

Yes, I want it. Oh yes, I do want it.

* * *

A klaxon sounding, a shout, another klaxon.

In the Boulevard Haussmann a middle-aged exporter of
French lace is following a woman. The automobiles roll
and jerk along the boulevard, the smell of petrol diluted
by clouds of perfume.

The exporter walks behind the woman. They pass
fashionable shops, mannequins, a languorous wooden
hand holding a wispy scarf, window shoppers, a schoolgirl skipping and laughing, then a fat woman rocking on
pointed heels, rocking like a metronome as she moves
from one shop window to the next.

The exporter is confident that the woman he follows
has no idea that he's following her. He stares at her back

as they walk. He stares at her prominent buttocks. She wears a red silk dress, her buttocks emphasized by the clinging silk. There is no way such a dress can hide those buttocks. She wants them displayed, doesn't she? She wants to be looked at. He imagines the white flesh rolling under the silk.

Now the woman stops to look in a shop window. The exporter stops behind her and he pretends to read a poster on a kiosk. The woman is so casual. No hurry at all. It's almost five o'clock and he was hoping for something more than a mere walk along the boulevard. He can see the bulge of her right breast and it excites him. Then a priest with a wide-brim hat blocks the exporter's view. The priest has rimless eyeglasses, a black briefcase in his right hand, his left hand on his belly. Now the priest transfers the briefcase from his right hand to his left hand and he raises a thin forefinger to scratch his nose.

The exporter looks away. He focuses his eyes on the poster, on the letter A, and now he realizes for the first time that his mouth is dry. His tongue seems to have grown immense and he has the feeling that if he opens his mouth his tongue will drop out like a heavy stone.

The priest moves on.

The woman is walking again.

The exporter follows three meters behind the woman, his eyes on her buttocks, on her silk-covered calves and then on her buttocks again.

My God, it's a view, he thinks. She wants it. Oh yes, she does want it.

* * *

Vita laughs.

—Well, you're a surprise, aren't you, darling?

—I think I was drugged.

—No, you weren't drugged. At least not in the ordinary

way. Yes, you're quite a surprise.

Vita teases Hilary as Hilary turns her face away. The people in the café continue chattering in the midst of the teasing. Yes, it was fun, Hilary thinks. But she hates the amusement in Vita's eyes.

Now Vita reaches out to touch Hilary's wrist.

—Was his name Julien?

—Yes.

Vita's finger strokes Hilary's wrist.

—I do know him.

Are the patrons in the café looking at them now? Vita talks about the weather. She talks about a new play. Her voice rises and falls and rises again. Hilary listens to Vita's voice as Vita's voice blends into the noise of the crowded café. She doesn't know everything, Hilary thinks. I haven't told all my secrets.

Vita laughs again.

—It's lovely, darling. It's really lovely.

* * *

Shadows again.

In the Blair sitting-room, Walter and Hilary sit in the dust and silence.

Hilary looks at the carpet. She looks at the clock. Walter slowly turns his head and his eyes once again show his astonishment.

—Hilary, it's awful.

The twilight is deepening, the slivers of light from the shutters sliding into a grey nothingness.

—Yes, it's awful.

—I won't accept it.

—Yes, you will, won't you?

He continues his denial. He fingers the lapels of his dressing gown. They toss their admissions at each other. Hilary looks at the clock again, at that horrible clock on

the fake marble over the mantel. He's a naughty boy,
Hilary thinks. Walter is a naughty boy. I married a
naughty boy, didn't I? What does he expect now? Does
he expect to carry her off to the bedroom? She doesn't
care anymore. What she has now is a complete apathy
about whatever it is they have between them.

He babbles about the maid again.

—We'll sack the girl.

—I don't care.

—Hilary, it's only a maid, isn't it?

—You had a fine time with her, didn't you? She's not
the only one, is she? You mustn't lie, Walter. Really, you
mustn't lie to me.

Well, I won't have it anymore, Hilary thinks. She'll
make up her own mind about things. It's Paris, isn't it?
This is Paris and she'll make up her own mind. He can
have his amusements if he wants them.

Hilary shifts her body in her chair. Walter looks at her
again and then he turns his face away. They sit once
again in the silence, Walter twisting his hands. Is he
thinking of his mother? Oh dear, I do hate his mother.

—All right, Walter says.

—We'll do as we like.

—Yes. I'll find a place of my own, if you think it's
best.

—As you like, darling. Please do as you like.

Hilary looks at the clock again. She avoids looking at
Walter. She crosses her legs and she looks at the clock
again.

* * *

Marceline is exhibiting herself. She stands in a private
room in a restaurant near the quai d'Orsay, her dress
raised in back to show her buttocks to the man who sits at
the table. She wears no panties; her buttocks are bare

above her gartered stockings. The man says nothing as he
stares at the white globes.

Is this the same man as the one in the place d'Italie?
No, this is a different man. This man wears a monocle.
He adjusts the monocle now and then he leans forward to
look more closely at Marceline's exposed buttocks.

PART TWO

Parma Violets

In this corner a golden yellow is opposed to a bright red background.

Vita laughs.

—He's mad, isn't he?

And here vermilion in the light and an acid green in the shadows. The colors are laid out in flat planes, juxtaposed, glaring, in places bordered with black. Hilary's head is spinning as she stares at the woman with an orange face.

The studio is off the place Denfert-Rochereau, a huge loft with hardly any furniture, the paintings on the floor with their backs against the decrepit walls or hanging here and there in a scattered array as an afterthought.

—He's quite mad, Vita says again. They all want to be painted by him, but I think he's quite mad.

Hilary gazes at the wild colors. In one painting a woman wearing a large hat and nothing else sits at a small table holding one of her breasts in one hand as she stares out of the picture at the viewer. The woman's face is a bright green, with a slash of red for the lips and a yellow stripe along the length of her nose.

Insolent ease, Hilary thinks. He has such an insolent ease with his colors.

His name is Octave Boulu, his studio now filled with a crowd of society people. Boulu the fashionable portraitist, the painter in demand.

Vita laughs again.

—They say he's not even French.

Now another painting of a woman, a thin body, a pallor broken only by the red gash of her mouth, the woman only half-dressed, one small breast exposed, the red color of the nipple matching the red color of her lips. She wears a necklace of glittering jewels and her eyes look haunted.

—I shouldn't like to be painted by him, Vita says. He has the ability to make a woman look horrible.

They wander through the crowd. Vita knows many of the people who have come to look at Boulu's paintings. Before long Hilary finds herself alone. She doesn't mind it. She moves from painting to painting, amused by the nudes, her senses aroused by the vibrant colors.

—Do you like them, madame? Do they have your approval?

Hilary turns. He has a bold head, his eyes fixed on hers. He tilts his head as he repeats the question.

—Do you like them?

—Yes.

—I am Octave Boulu.

—Yes, I know.

He smiles as he begins to talk about his work. Hilary doesn't care about his work. She imagines she's a small girl again, a girl on a holiday in Providence. How silly it is to think of that. Boulu is not her father; Boulu is definitely not her father.

—You must call me Octave.

—All right.

His eyes are amused. He says he does not know many Americans. Does he think her a schoolgirl? Hilary gazes at his wet lips. She thinks of her mother. She wonders what her mother would say about these wild paintings of undressed women. Is the painter flirting with her? Yes, it's definitely a flirtation. He's talking nonsense now, rambling about the trees in the south of France. She feels herself measured by his eyes. He stares at her throat, at her shoulders, at her hips. He has such mastery in his eyes. His eyes make her quiver and Hilary wonders how

he manages it.
—Let's leave this place, Octave says.
—But these people are your guests.
—The hell with all of them. My dealer can look after things.

* * *

He has her in a restaurant, in a private room. The room has no windows and Hilary feels a clutch of anxiety in her chest. Who is this man? Why is she here with him? He's quiet now. He engages his food. He sips the red wine. Hilary wonders if he's putting on an act for her. They sit side by side on a bench and he turns to look at her only occasionally. His eyes are vacant. She sees nothing in his eyes. He disregards her. Does he think he owns her? Has she become a possession of Octave Boulu? When Hilary looks at his face, she finds she can see nothing but his wet mouth, his wet lips. She wonders what he's like; she wonders about his needs. Everyone has their needs, don't they? He has the hands of an artist, expressive hands, the fingers almost delicate. He seems not to care about money but he has expensive tastes. Once again he gazes at Hilary's throat, at her bare arms. The waiter glides into the room, fusses a bit with something on the table and then glides out again. Octave sips the red wine and he begins eating again.

* * *

Now a taxi in the Bois.
Oh yes, he's well-bred. Octave is a man of breeding, a Parisian aristocrat. Hilary sits beside him in the rear of the taxi, close enough beside him so that their knees touch as she looks at the woods in the twilight. Octave murmurs occasionally. Is the driver listening? Then Octave places his right hand upon Hilary's left knee and

he squeezes the knee with his fingers.
—Are you content?
—Yes.
—You're a strange woman, aren't you?
—No, I don't think so.
—I was once a waiter in Les Halles.
—I can't imagine it.
Octave laughs.
—But it's true.
He's a perfect gentleman. He takes her hand now and
he kisses it. He runs his wet lips over fingers and then
over her palm. He tickles her palm with his mouth. Then
he talks again about his paintings. Yes, the driver is
listening to them. Hilary can see the driver's head cocked
to one side in his listening. Octave talks and talks. I don't
understand it, Hilary thinks. I don't understand what he
says to me. Octave's hand is on her knees again, his
fingers stroking her knees as he gently pushes her legs
apart.

What does he want? It's crazy, Hilary thinks. Then a
shudder passes through her as Octave leans toward her
and kisses her neck above the collar of her dress.

He touches her breasts. Hilary has a sudden thought to
prevent it, but she does nothing except close her eyes.
She sits there beside Octave with her eyes closed as his
fingers roam over the contours of her breasts. Then he
covers her right breast with all of his hand, the hand
pressing her breast through the clothes that cover it.

Can anyone see them? Hilary opens her eyes now to
look at the Bois through the window. She sees nothing
but shadows among the trees. She thinks of the dinner in
that restaurant, Octave sipping the red wine.

Now he gently pushes her knees apart. The hand is
gone from her breast, but now the hand is between her
knees. Does she feel any surprise? Octave is touching her
thighs above the tops of her stockings.

I'm a dignified woman, Hilary thinks. But here she sits
in a taxi with Octave's hand between her thighs. She feels
his fingers walking along the soft skin on the insides of
her thighs.

You must behave properly, she thinks. Hilary, darling,
you must behave properly.

Octave does not behave properly. He finds the joining
of her thighs, her mount swollen under the silk knickers,
her wet sex.

Hilary shudders as Octave's fingers push into the folds
of her wet sex.

—The pink mouth, Octave says.

—Octave, please. . .

—In every woman the pink is different.

—Oh God.

—I must paint it soon.

—Octave, the driver. . . Octave removes his fingers
from her sex and he orders the driver to take them out of
the Bois.

* * *

He has a charming house on the Ile Saint-Louis. An
old valet opens the door, looks at Hilary with a hint of
arrogance. The house is rich in its luxuries. The society
people that Octave paints have made him rich. A maid
arrives to open the shutters in the drawing-room. Hilary
avoids the eyes of the maid. The old valet serves them
brandy and Hilary avoids the eyes of the valet. She
ignores the brandy. She stands near an open window and
she looks at the lights along the quai de Bourbon.

When the valet leaves, Octave brings Hilary her
brandy. He says nothing to her. He sips the brandy in his
glass with his left hand and he puts his right hand on her
buttocks.

Hilary freezes under his touch. Dear girl, what do you

want? she thinks. You need to be honest about things.
You need a touch of honesty, darling.

—You're trembling, Octave says.

—Yes.

His fingertips move slowly over the rounds of her buttocks. The dress she wears, the underthings, are thin
enough so that she feels each movement of the exploring
fingers. He examines the curves of her buttocks, his
fingers measuring the curves, his fingertips stroking the
curves as they stand there in front of the open window
that looks out on a small street off the quai de Bourbon.

—Sit down now.

Hilary turns from the window. She glances at the door.
Yes, the door is closed. She sits down in a beechwood
armchair ornamented with elaborate carvings. The uphol-
stery is firm. Her legs are still trembling. She crosses her
legs. Octave is talking to her, but she understands nothing
of what he says and she avoids looking at him. She senses
his approach, and now when she does look at him she
discovers that he has his organ exposed.

Octave's penis protrudes out of the opening of his
trousers, curved and pink, swaying under Hilary's astonished eyes, twitching like an impatient serpent.

Hilary stares at Octave's organ.

Like the man, she thinks. The curve is an affectation,
the arcing of the shaft an affectation of force.

—Suck the tip, Octave says. Only the tip of it.

His voice is flat, not a trace of excitement in his voice
as he pushes his knob against Hilary's lips. She does what
he wants. She opens her lips just enough to get the tip of
his knob inside her mouth. It's the first time. Vita said:
Haven't you ever? This is the first time. Hilary has the
taste of Octave's organ on her tongue. She has a tantaliz-
ing scent in her nose, the smell of Octave's penis floating
through her nose and then deep inside her brain. He
doesn't move. She has no more than half his knob

covered with her lips. Dear God, I'm doing this, she
thinks. She can't imagine herself doing it, but this is
definitely Octave's penis in her mouth. His flesh is warm
between her lips. Nothing is doubted now; she has no
doubt about what she's doing.

Octave pushes forward a bit.

Hilary knows what he wants. She opens her mouth to
accept his knob. Octave continues pushing forward, his
knob and his shaft sliding over Hilary's tongue, sliding
smoothly over Hilary's tongue as she widens her mouth
to accommodate the girth of his organ.

Then he pulls back a bit and he holds himself motionless again, this time with his shaft stretching her lips into
a round exclamation. Hilary remembers the roundness of
the lips of the girl in Madame Mathilde's establishment.
She remembers the girl's red lips. Are my lips as red as
the lips of that girl?

Octave slowly pulls his organ completely out of
Hilary's mouth.

—You have an exquisite mouth.

He makes her rise from the chair. Hilary rises in a
daze. Octave moves against her. He kisses her wet
mouth. She feels a sudden burning intimacy, a new bond
between her and the painter. When he pulls his lips away
from hers, his face is impassive. Hilary stands motionless
as he slowly lifts her dress. She remembers Octave's studio and the party of society people gazing at his wild
paintings. Now Octave is gazing at her thighs, at the garters that hold up her stockings, at her pink silk drawers
with a lace frill at the edge that now makes her feel so
awkward.

Octave has her hold her dress at her hips while he
walks to a table, opens a drawer and returns to her with a
pair of small scissors in his hand. Hilary feels a sudden
dismay, a sudden fear of the scissors. But Octave reas-
sures her. He strokes her chin. Then he drops his hand

and he strokes the lace edges of her knickers. Then a moment later he begins cutting at the silk with the scissors, cutting and snipping and pulling at her knickers until he has most of the front cut away to expose the bush of hair at the joining of her thighs.

Hilary feels a desperation again. She tells herself she ought to rebel against it. She tells herself she ought to make her protest now before it's much too late.

She does nothing. She closes her eyes at the moment she feels Octave's fingers in her sex. He explores her. He pulls at the petals. Hilary is petrified with embarrassment because she knows how drenched she is. She remains immobile as Octave continues to finger her little jewel. My little bijou, Hilary thinks. His touch is deft. He has her shuddering. Again and again his fingertip strokes her clitoris. Hilary feels the imminence of the explosion. She's afraid again. She's afraid the universe will explode inside her eyes.

Octave suddenly removes his fingers.

Hilary shudders. She hangs on the edge of a precipice, without orgasm, without completion.

He makes her sit down again in the beechwood armchair. Hilary understands nothing; she does what he wants; she sits in the chair without comprehension. Are there reasons for anything? Octave drops to his knees and he spreads Hilary's legs. He spreads her legs and he studies her. Hilary sits there trembling as Octave gazes at her sex. His face is impassive. He opens her sex with his fingers and his face is still impassive. Then he lifts her legs to his shoulders, her silk-covered legs sliding over Octave's shoulders. Yes, she wants it. Hilary shifts her body forward on the chair. She fixes her eyes on Octave's mouth and she watches his wet lips as they approach her sex.

How absurd, Hilary thinks. One mouth against the other. Two pairs of lips touching in a secret kiss. Even as she watches the kiss, it remains secret. She feels his tongue in her groove, Octave's tongue between the swollen lips of her sex. She looks down at him. She feels the heat in her face. He licks her clitoris with the very tip of his tongue, up and down along the shaft of her clitoris, up and down that pink bauble, up and down with a continual rasping of his tongue that drives Hilary towards an inevitable madness.

Oh God now, she thinks.

She throws her head back as she cries out. Octave holds her thighs with his hands as he burrows in to suck at the running fountain. He continues to suck as her body trembles through one spasm after another. Then finally it's finished, Hilary drained and exhausted. When she opens her eyes, she sees Octave dabbing at his mouth with a white handkerchief. His organ is hidden again, his trousers buttoned and his clothes in order. Hilary quickly covers her thighs with her dress.

—I want you to pose for me, Octave says. Will you pose for me?

—I don't know.

—Where is your husband?

—In London, I think. We don't see much of each other.

—Tomorrow we'll have lunch together. Would you like that?

—Yes.

* * *

These two gentleman are walking in the Tuileries, one with a white boater hat and a grey suit, the other with a dark bowler hat and a dark suit. They both have moustaches; the man wearing the bowler hat has a short beard. They both carry dark leather briefcases.

The man in the boater hat rubs his moustache.

—She's quite good, you know. Elegant when she has

the right clothes.
—What's her name?
—Marceline.
—Does she whine? I don't like it when they whine. I
don't like it when they're always begging for presents.
—No, she's quite good. She knows how to behave.
—You're being too nice to me.
The man in the boater hat laughs.
—It's a favor, isn't it?

2.

In the morning Hilary lies in her own bed, an empty
bed, an empty room, the sun brilliant as it filters through
the cracks in the shutters. Hilary lies in her bed alone.
She turns slowly, turns from her side to lie on her back in
a quiet languor.

He refused, didn't he? Octave refused to make love to
her. Hilary remembers his organ, his penis vibrating. But
he refused. She suddenly wonders about Walter. Where
is Walter now? The flat is empty of Walter's things. Then
she thinks of Jack and Arthur. Walter's chums. Does
Walter know? She refuses to see them again. They beg
and she refuses. What a farce it is. How confusing it is. I
don't want the confusion, Hilary thinks. She wets her
lips. She thinks about leaving the bed but she remains
motionless. What a lark with Octave. She remembers the
feel of his mouth pressing against her sex. She
remembers the heat of his organ between her lips. And
then his refusal.

It's the sun again. It's now more brilliant than ever in
the room. Hilary raises her left leg and then she lowers
it. She covers her eyes with her forearm and then she

removes the arm to look at the room again.

She thinks of Octave's refusal. She thinks of his eyes, his mouth, his fingers as they explored her sex. She thinks of the curve of his organ. That sceptre.

Walter could never imagine it. Hilary is certain Walter could never imagine her with a man like Octave Boulu. Well, Walter is gone, isn't he? He's left her the flat and enough to live on, but he's completely gone.

Gone, Hilary thinks. Walter is gone and now I have Octave.

I do have Octave, don't I?

* * *

Octave has Hilary in a taxi again. She sits beside Octave in the rear of a taxi as it crawls along the Boulevard Haussmann. Octave talks, but Hilary pays no attention to his words. She quivers as she feels Octave's hand fondling her knees. What a precious day it is. What precious days these are. Hilary looks at the pedestrians on the sidewalks. She wonders if they notice her, if they notice her sitting beside Octave. She wonders if they imagine things. Octave now has his hand between Hilary's thighs, his fingers rubbing her stockings, her garters, the tender skin of her thighs above the tops of her stockings.

I am not envious of women, Hilary thinks. I don't envy them. Women are not to be envied.

Octave's fingers are persistent. She hates it when he treats her like a tart. Don't you hate it, Hilary? His fingers are touching the silk of her drawers. She's wetting herself. She knows she's wetting the leather of the seat and she hates that too. What a scandal it is. How awful to have it done in a taxi like this. Hilary is certain the pedestrians on the boulevard are looking at them. Hilary shudders as Octave's fingertip strokes her clitoris. Hilary closes her eyes and she pretends that the Boulevard

Haussmann has suddenly ceased to exist.

* * *

The quai de Bourbon sparkles in the sunlight. From the open window in Octave's drawing room, one can see the Pont Marie and a barge as it now slowly vanishes under one of the arches of the bridge. The stones of the bridge have an ochre color, the shadows a mixture of grey and bluish-green.

The clock on the mantel makes a delicate sound as it strikes the hour.

Hilary and Octave are motionless, both fully dressed, Octave standing with the front of his trousers unbuttoned, Hilary seated before Octave with his organ in her mouth.

She has the feel of the man in her mouth. She remains motionless as Octave starts to move. Then Hilary moves her lips and she begins a slow sucking of his penis.

No escape, Hilary thinks. She has his flesh in her mouth and now there is no escape.

Octave murmurs something. He strokes her face to offer his encouragement. Hilary wonders if she ought to be surprised. She feels the heat of his flesh with her lips and tongue. Octave makes a sound of pleasure in his throat. He touches her head with both hands now and Hilary understands his meaning. She waits for it. She waits for Octave's spasm. Then the moment arrives and Hilary trembles as she feels the jetting of Octave's sperm on her tongue. Octave shudders as he finishes. Hilary swallows his offering, and then Octave completes the consecration by stroking her face again.

* * *

On another day Octave takes Hilary to his studio and there he makes her pose for him. Hilary is frightened by a cluster of dried lilies in a black vase. She stands in

front of a large violet drapery. She wears her jewelry, a
necklace of pearls, two bracelets on each wrist, her rings.
She wears her shoes and stockings, now rolled above her
knees, but otherwise her body is naked. Octave tells her
to roll the stockings down to her ankles. Hilary bends to
do what he wants. Then she stands again. She stands
with her hands at her sides, her ankles pressed one
against the other, her thighs and legs pressed one against
the other, her face turned just a bit to the left, to the light
that falls on her breasts and belly.

—Perfect, Octave says.

—Will it take long?

—Haven't you ever posed before?

—Never like this.

—Don't move now. I won't do more than a sketch
today.

Afterwards he offers Hilary a cigarette. Then he wants
her to parade for him. He wants her to walk about the
studio just as she is. He says he finds her nakedness cap-
tivating.

Hilary walks for Octave. She tells herself she has no
hope anymore. When she approaches Octave again, he
kisses her and he fondles her buttocks. Hilary stands
there quietly while he explores the texture of her skin.
How many minutes? Hilary has the feeling that a
thousand minutes have passed while Octave strokes her
buttocks. Then he makes her parade again, this time more
slowly, back and forth in front of him. He talks about
conventions. Hilary feels the movement of her breasts as
she walks back and forth in front of Octave.

Then he stops her and he kisses her again. His hand is
more insistent as he fondles her buttocks. Hilary blushes
as she feels the probing of his fingers. Octave rubs his
lips against hers as he mumbles, as he describes his fasci-
nation with her body. Hilary shudders as she feels his
fingertips pushing against her anus. She has a sudden

memory of a collection of lewd photographs shown to her at a drunken party in New York.

—I want you here, Octave says.

—What?

—The little one. It's quite good, isn't it?

Hilary remembers the girl at Madame Mathilde's.

—I don't know. I've never. . .

Octave chuckles.

—Never?

—No, never.

Hilary notices a newspaper on one of the chairs. The newspapers are filled with reviews of the new exposition of decorative arts. This is one of those summers in Paris when life seems to be the finest thing imaginable. Hilary looks down and sees that Octave's organ is exposed. I must recognize myself, Hilary thinks. I do need to recognize myself. She drops to her knees and she takes Octave's penis in her mouth. She sucks on the knob of Octave's penis as she wonders what Walter would think. He'd think her mad, no doubt. But Octave is a celebrity, isn't he? All the women in Paris are after him to paint their portraits.

Octave makes her stand up again.

—You do want it, don't you?

Hilary shrugs.

—I don't know.

—You must say you want it.

She holds his organ in her hand. She feels the heat of his flesh with her fingers.

—Yes, I want it.

Octave laughs.

—I don't believe you.

—Please, Octave, I do want it.

He has her bend over a small table. Hilary suddenly imagines she hears applause from somewhere. Then a shudder passes through her body as she feels the wood of the table against her face. Octave has undressed now. He comes behind her and she feels his fingers between her buttocks. She feels him oiling her, an oil of some kind, oiling her anus with his fingertips.

Hilary quivers. Are you afraid, darling? You do want it, don't you? She doesn't know. She never knows, does she? It's always the same. Darkness and light and then darkness again.

She feels him. She feels his knob pushing at her. She feels each movement as he pushes at her oiled opening. Her eyes are closed now. Yes, she's afraid. Her legs tremble as she feels the penetration of his organ.

—You're a healthy woman, Octave says. You're taking it quite well.

—Octave, please. . .

—Don't move yet.

—It hurts.

—The hurt will pass.

The pain is already turning to a dull ache and then slowly vanishing. Hilary keeps her eyes closed. She's afraid that if she opens her eyes she'll find herself in front of an audience. She thinks she hears the applause again. Dear God, it's madness. She feels a great yielding now, a hot submission of her body to Octave's penetration.

Octave mumbles something as he pushes forward again.

He's greedy, Hilary thinks. He wants everything, doesn't he?

Then she feels him moving again and she moans against the wood of the table.

* * *

—You're a modest woman, Octave says.

Hilary shifts her body on the chaise; she avoids his eyes.

—Is that a fault?

—It's a scourge, an affliction of the Church. Have you looked at my paintings? If I make the sex too well-defined, they tell me the paintings will be confiscated. What they want is a stupid pretense of something 'that doesn't exist. They want a woman without a sex. So I paint the portraits of these society bitches and I become rich. It's a farce, isn't it? They confiscate the paintings and then afterwards they find their little mistresses to look at the real thing. They want the sex hidden. They want the pretense.

—Am I your little mistress?

—You're my little bonbon.

—You hurt me.

—I told you, the hurt will pass.

* * *

One afternoon they take the road south to the park at Sceaux. Octave says he has a revived interest in the outskirts of Paris. He says these days Paris has become too congested for an orderly life. Hilary sits beside Octave in the rear of a hired car. She sits close to him, close enough so that her left thigh makes contact with his right thigh. She looks forward to the picnic in the park. Such a long time has passed since she's had a lunch on the grass. Hilary, darling, do you know what you want? She gazes at the trees that line the straight road. Now she remembers that drive to Versailles with Walter. Well, this isn't Walter, is it? Now she has Octave Boulu beside her in the rear of a car. He's a villain, isn't he? Oh yes, he's a villain, all right. Octave moves his right arm now, and in a moment he has his hand between Hilary's thighs. Hilary tells herself it's a question of circumstance. All of her life has been a question of circumstance. The painter Octave Boulu is toying with her knickers. She feels his fingers. She feels him tickling the lips of her sex through the silk of her knickers. It's a question of circumstance, isn't it? Hilary closes her eyes as Octave continues tickling her with his fingertips.

Then finally they arrive at the old park and Octave orders the driver to stop. Hilary walks with Octave to the edge of a wood. They spread the blanket and open the picnic basket beneath a large tree. Hilary feels like a young girl again. She laughs as Octave pours the red wine. Octave questions Hilary about her childhood. Hilary tells herself that such a long time has passed since her childhood. Is the driver of the hired car sleeping? Octave is now complaining about all the clochards in Paris. Too many derelicts in the streets. Octave drinks a great deal of the red wine. Hilary wishes they were in the Luxembourg instead of here in the Sceaux. Then she looks at Octave and she sees that he has his organ exposed. Hilary blushes as she stares at the pink knob of Octave's penis.

—Do you like it? Octave says.

—Yes.

—All true women like the penis. Perhaps even the lesbians.

—I don't know.

—You must meet Nora Gale sometime.

—Is she a lesbian?

Octave laughs, his fingers stroking his organ.

—But yes, Nora Gale is certainly a lesbian.

He wants Hilary to suck his penis. Hilary glances quickly at the car fifty yards away near the road, and then she lowers her head to Octave's lap to take his penis in her mouth.

Octave sighs as she sucks his organ. Hilary thinks of idols, Oriental idols like those huge statues that one sees in the photographs of Indo-China. She sucks at the fruit-like knob of Octave's penis. She imagines herself a slave girl, an exotic creature wearing baroque jewels and living in a temple somewhere. Octave sighs again as Hilary slides her lips back and forth over the swollen flesh of his knob.

After a while Octave pulls at Hilary's dress to expose her thighs and buttocks. She lies there with her head in his lap and her hips uncovered. He strokes her buttocks through her knickers. He says her underthings are too chaste, too ordinary. Hilary wriggles as Octave removes her knickers. Now he strokes her buttocks with his hand. She would rather he touched her breasts instead. She lies still with his penis in her mouth as she waits for him. He tickles the crack between her buttocks without penetrating her. Hilary trembles. Octave's fingers are more real than the fingers of any man she has ever known. She's happy he has her knickers down. She adores the way his hand measures the curving of her hip.

—Can you find the marmalade? Octave says.

Hilary reaches for the jar of marmalade and she hands it to Octave. In a moment she feels his fingers in the crack between her buttocks again. The marmalade. Hilary shudders as Octave applies the marmalade to the ring of her anus. She feels a sudden revulsion as Octave's finger-tip penetrates her bottom.

On her knees now. Hilary has her head down and her face pressed against the wool of the blanket. She can feel the grass under the blanket, the blades of grass flattened by her cheek.

Then she quivers as she feels Octave's knob pushing inside her bottom. Dear God, I don't want it, Hilary thinks. Don't you like it, darling? She wonders if the driver is looking at them. Hilary imagines the driver's eyes can see everything. She feels the blood pounding in her ears. She hears Octave mumbling something. It's only at times like this that he ever shows any genuine emotion. Hilary moans. My life has come to this, she thinks.

Octave speaks again.

—You enjoy it, don't you?

Hilary shudders. How disturbing he is. She keeps her eyes closed.

—You must tell me, Octave says.

—Octave, please. . .

—You must tell me. You do like it, don't you?

—Yes.

He laughs.

—You're an exquisite woman. Beautifully made. Quite beautifully made.

She feels the stretching again, the forcing, the pushing and the presence of his organ in her bottom. She wonders if it's an error to give herself like this. Then she trembles as she feels his organ moving again. I don't know, Hilary thinks. How is a woman to judge these things? She's now quite certain that she'll do anything Octave asks of her.

* * *

A drawing-room off the quai d'Anjou. The man is in evening dress, four points of a white handkerchief in his breast pocket, dark hair flat on his skull, a high forehead, a thin face, large eyes bulging beneath dark brows.

The woman stands at the window with her back to the room, her face seen in profile, the cheek heavily rouged, lips glistening and red, her skin shimmering beneath a diaphanous gown, a pink gown, in places a floral design, buttocks and thighs visible and shadowed, her waist flowing smoothly up to the open expanse of her back and shoulders.

—You don't understand, she says.

Now she turns and she faces the room, a shadow beneath her belly, a shadow at the point of each breast. The man remains standing with his back to the woman, his eyes locked on a stuccoed wall.

—I want to begin something, the woman says.

—The train, the man says. The train leaves at six. Or is it seven, I really don't remember.

—Why don't you open the door? It's not my fault the weather is awful.

—It must be six. If the train leaves at seven it will arrive much too late.

—I really would like to know what you think of this. It's transparent. The latest fashion.

—I'll have a cigar. That's a good idea, isn't it? I'll have a Cuban cigar.

3.

Quite certain? Are you quite certain, Hilary?

She sits with Octave in a café, her head in a tangle of memories. Where is she? Is she still Mrs. Hilary Blair? I don't want to be a mature woman, Hilary thinks. The deep source of my problem is that I don't want to be a mature woman.

Does Octave think she's a mature woman? Octave now has his hand on her knee, his fingers pressing her kneecap beneath the café table. The café is crowded and Hilary sits close to Octave on the cushion of the bench. She has the awful feeling that people are staring at them, staring at her legs and staring at Octave's hand as it holds her left knee.

You're a fool, Hilary. These people don't care about you. That woman over there, the one with thick red lips, that woman is busy thinking about the death of her pet cat.

Octave now pushes at Hilary's knees to get them apart. She's wearing open knickers, the crotch taken out by

Octave's scissors, and she trembles as she does his bidding. She moves her legs apart, a slow movement of her thighs, a slow opening to the deeper shadows.

That boy is looking at her. But then he looks away and Hilary breathes again.

Octave's hand moves higher between Hilary's thighs. She feels his fingertips. She feels the touching of her sex. He turns to face her now. He leans against her, kisses her ear as his thumb finds her clitoris. He rolls her clitoris as one of his fingers enters the opening below it.

Hilary shudders.

Octave whispers.

—Are you coming?

—Yes.

It doesn't happen that often, does it? She needs to be touched in just the right way. Octave has such an immense power to make her enjoy it. He strokes her clitoris with his thumb as his thick middle finger moves inside her sex. Hilary bites her lip. That boy is looking at her again. That boy is looking at her and Hilary is certain the boy has guessed what's happening to her.

Oh God.

Octave removes his fingers. He pays the bill and he leads Hilary out of the café.

—I'm famished, Octave says. It's time for a good dinner.

They ride in a taxi to a restaurant in a narrow street, a place as crowded as the café, a place where Octave hails the manager and immediately secures a table in a corner. The waiter arrives with a great flourish of his long apron.

Well, it's impressive, Hilary thinks. Octave is something impressive, isn't he?

The patrons are looking at them. Hilary blushes as she remembers Octave's fingers in her sex. Her head is swimming as she sips the white wine that Octave has ordered. Now once again Octave has his hand on her knee. Does he wonder what she has in her mind when she feels his fingers there?

—Open your legs, Octave says.

Hilary thinks of her marriage as she opens her legs to Octave's hand. She wonders if any of the patrons can see that her sex is exposed, her bush uncovered by the opening in her knickers.

The gate, Hilary thinks. It's the gate to everything, isn't it?

She imagines the eyes of the patrons have found her little gate. She trembles as she imagines the eyes of the patrons.

* * *

Vita turns the curls of blonde hair that hang over her right temple. Hilary turns the glass of Pernod and she wonders what Vita thinks. It's always so difficult to know what Vita thinks. They sit here surrounded by people, surrounded by the crowd at the Café Dome.

I don't like crowds, Hilary thinks. There was a time when she did like crowds, but now she doesn't. She feels like a prisoner in the midst of a herd of animals.

—I'm having a fling with Octave Boulu, Hilary says.

Vita laughs.

—You're teasing me.

—But it's true.

Hilary tells Vita about her affair with Octave. Is Vita envious? Hilary tells herself that now she's more sophisticated than Vita. I want her to be envious. I do want her to be envious.

Vita presses for details.

—You must tell me everything.

—It's much too bizarre.

Vita laughs.

—Oh, I do love that word.

Hilary feels in a fine mood. She deliberately teases
Vita. She tells the blonde just enough to maintain a certain level of excitement in Vita's eyes.

Vita lifts her chin with a new respect.

—Did he really cut your knickers?

—Yes.

—How ghastly.

—No, it was quite nice.

—An experience, I should say.

—Yes, an experience.

* * *

Octave pays a visit to Hilary's flat. Hilary offers him
wine and she quivers as she considers the possibilities.
Then Octave begins talking about his former mistresses
and Hilary is dismayed. She listens. Of course she never
expected to be the first. She listens to his mumblings and
she wonders about the others. The other women. I don't
like Paris. It's like a hothouse, isn't it? All these people
sweltering like orchids. You're jealous, darling. You're
jealous of all these other women he's had. Hilary feels
weak. She feels as though she's falling. Is Octave leading
her away? Hilary finds herself on her bed. She lies there
naked on her bed as Octave hovers over her like a dark
cloud. He kisses the top of her head. She feels his fingers
in her sex. She feels his hands raising her legs in the air.
She feels his knob pushing inside her grotto. Octave
penetrates her sex. His organ burrows in her sex like an
eager mole. She hears him grunting as he finishes. She
feels the wetness. She quivers as she feels the wetness.

A taste of peppermint, Hilary. You have a taste of peppermint on your tongue.

* * *

Hilary continues posing for Octave in his studio.

Am I a lotus-eater? Hilary stares at the skylight as she poses for him. The studio smells of paint and tobacco and incense.

Now he wants her in a chair. Hilary is naked; she wears nothing but a pair of dangling earrings. She moves to the armchair and she arranges herself according to Octave's instructions. He wants her sex exposed. The little rabbit, he calls it. Hilary opens her legs to his eyes. She wishes the afternoon to end. She wishes for the quiet of the night. She trembles as Octave begins working at his easel again. What an awful moment, Hilary thinks. She hates it when he has her exposed like this. But of course the excitement is there. You fancy it, don't you, darling? Hilary trembles as Octave mixes his paints.

*   *   *

One day Hilary waits for Octave in a café, her eyes on the procession of pedestrians on the boulevard. She waits for Octave and she ignores the glances of the men around her. She's completely obsessed with Octave these days. The line has been passed. The men around her have ceased to exist for her. She waits for Octave; she waits for the moments of quiet frenzy.

But this afternoon when Octave arrives, he has a friend with him. A slender man with sad eyes.

Well, at least it's not a girl, Hilary thinks.

His name is Jan. A Dutch painter. They smile at each other. Octave says that Jan's paintings will be cherished by the future. The two men chuckle at each other about something. They order wine. Hilary is aware of Jan's eyes, the way he stares at her. Now she wonders what the women around her are thinking. Can she have two husbands? She finds herself between two men. Is it Hilary who possesses the men or is it the men who possess Hilary?

After they leave the café, they go to Octave's studio. Octave is talking about one of the dealers, waving his arm in the air as he talks. Hilary now regrets the presence of Jan. As they climb the stairs to Octave's studio, Hilary hopes that Jan will leave them. She has no interest in the Dutch painter. She has no interest in Jan and his paintings.

Inside the studio, Octave wants Hilary to pose for him.

—It's a good time to work. I'm in the mood to work again. We'll do the standing portrait.

In the standing portrait, Hilary is nude.

—But Jan is here.

Octave laughs.

Jan pulls at his blonde moustache.

Hilary goes behind the screen to remove her clothes.

When she comes out into the open space of the studio again, the men are quiet. Octave is at his easel. Jan is in a chair with a pipe in his hand.

Hilary assumes the pose in front of the large expanse of drapery. Is Jan gallant? Is it his gallantry she feels? She stands there with her hands at her sides, her breasts trembling. How awful to be undressed like this. Then she admits to herself that she likes it. Yes, she likes it. You do like it, don't you, Hilary? She's aware of the eyes of the men. Octave at his easel and Jan in his chair. She's curious to know what Jan thinks. What does he think of her body? Does he find her breasts pleasing to his eyes? Octave always says she has bold nipples. She wonders what Jan thinks as he considers her nipples.

Octave talks as he works. Hilary gazes at the far wall. It's not any different with Jan in the studio. She hears them talking in another language. Is it Dutch? Then the talking stops and Octave comes out from behind the easel to approach Hilary.

—That's enough, eh?

He has his organ exposed, his penis extended out of the

opening in his trousers. Hilary stares at it. The resemblance to a serpent is always frightening. Then she
remember the presence of Jan and a shudder passes
through her body.

—Octave, please. . .

—Jan and I are old friends.

Hilary tells herself that her life is finished. She allows
Octave to lead her to an empty chair. She sits. She closes
her eyes and she turns her face away from Octave. His
fingers touch her chin and she faces him again. She faces
his organ, the pink serpent wavering in front of her eyes.
Octave moves forward and he pushes the knob of his
penis at Hilary's lips. Hilary does what he wants. She
opens her mouth and she begins the sucking of his organ.

With exactness. Octave has told her that she's quite
adept at it now. She rolls her lips over the knob, behind
the knob, along the shaft and then back again to the tip.

She does not want to look at Jan. She knows that Jan's
eyes are watching her and she does not want to look at
him.

Octave talks again as Hilary sucks his penis. He talks
to Jan.

—Crank up the phonograph.

The phonograph? Hilary shudders as she feels Octave's
penis swelling in her mouth. She prays he won't finish
now. She prays he won't make her swallow his sperm
while Jan is watching them.

Hilary's prayer is answered. Octave pulls his wet penis
out of Hilary's mouth. He takes her hand and he makes
her rise and now he leads her to the chaise near the wall.

You're a poor little girl, Hilary thinks. What a pity it is
that you're a poor little girl.

Octave poses her on the chaise. He arranges her body.
Then he laughs as he quickly strips his clothes away.

—You're an enchantment.

—Octave, please. . .

He bends to kiss her mouth. He mounts her, his body
between her thighs, his organ pushing at her sex, pushing
and entering and sliding forward.

Music now. It's a violin, isn't it? Is it Brahms or Men-
delssohn?

Hilary shudders. Her mind swims in its confusion. She
closes her eyes as Octave completes the penetration of
her sex. Then she opens her eyes and she sees Octave
smiling at her, his mouth stretched, his teeth.

Octave is more excited than usual. Is it the presence of
Jan?

Be practical, Hilary. Darling, you must be practical.

She knows Jan is looking at them. She feels Jan's eyes
as Octave once again pushes at her with his blunt
weapon.

The sound of the violin floats out of the horn of the
phonograph.

I want to be somewhere else, Hilary thinks. But where,
darling? Where is it you want to be? This is Octave's
studio, isn't it? This is Paris, isn't it? This is the studio
of Octave Boulu in Paris.

Octave continues thrusting.

Hilary now prays for a bed. She hates it when he takes
her like this. She hates the tangle of limbs, the pressing
of her body against the back of the chaise, the awkward
bending of her legs.

Don't be absurd, Hilary. It doesn't do any good to be
absurd.

She reaches for Octave now. She slides a hand along
her belly and down to her sex. She finds his thrusting
penis. She finds his balls and she holds them. She holds
his fat balls in her hand as he continues thrusting at her.

Octave calls out to Jan. The words mean nothing to
Hilary. She holds Octave's balls as she turns her head to
look at the Dutch painter.

Jan is naked. His body is a blur of pink. He has a long

organ that dangles over his pink testicles. He smiles at Hilary as he approaches the chaise.

Octave continues thrusting, his organ sliding back and forth in Hilary's sex.

Hilary stares at Jan's long penis. Her head rocks each time Octave pushes against her. Is she surprised? She keeps her eyes fixed on the swaying of Jan's penis. His bold organ. Hilary extends her free hand to fondle Jan's penis. Then she holds Jan's balls. Yes, why not? She has Octave's balls in her left hand and Jan's balls in her right hand. She feels the weight of their testicles. The coarse hair. The men are talking to each other. They make odd gestures with their hands. Hilary pulls Jan closer to the chaise. She abandons his testicles and instead she takes hold of his penis. She lifts his knob to her mouth, Jan's pink knob between her lips. Jan shudders as he feels Hilary's teeth. Hilary sucks Jan's organ while Octave continues thrusting.

She has both men. Dear God, what a memory, Hilary thinks. What a thing to remember. One moment she feels excitement and the next moment she feels the old revulsion. The end is near. Hilary can sense the end is near, time running out, the men at the edge of their conclusions.

Octave is the first. He makes a hissing sound as he has his spasm. Hilary wants to turn to watch his face, but she has Jan's organ in her mouth and all she can do is move her eyes. How strange it is to look at Octave while she has Jan's penis in her mouth.

Now Jan. The Dutchman grunts as he completes his pleasure. Hilary feels the warm flood of Jan's sperm on her tongue. She suddenly thinks of Walter. She suddenly imagines her husband watching this mad performance.

It's madness, Hilary thinks. It's complete madness. She swallows what Jan has given her. First excitement and then the nausea. Revulsion again, complete revulsion.

Oh yes, it's madness.

* * *

Marceline is with two girlfriends in a bar in Montmartre. The girls are laughing at something. They stand at the bar, Marceline in the center, each girl with a petit vin rouge on the bar in front of her hands.

—I've had it, Marceline says. It's too dead here. I'm going to Deauville.

—Deauville? Why Deauville?

—Because it's by the sea and it's busy. And next month it's the racing season and it's even better.

—There's too much competition, darling.

—Too many English.

Marceline shrugs.

—It's all the same, isn't it? If you put them side by side, there's no difference.

The two girls laugh.

—All right, we'll go with you.

4.

Octave's portrait of Hilary is finished. Hilary has agreed to allow him to offer the painting for sale at one of the galleries. Yes, why not? She can't imagine having it at home. She stands nude in the painting, rather vacant looking, her hands awkwardly at her sides and her appearance that of a surprised strumpet with her stockings rolled at her ankles. Hilary now regrets the painting, the circumstances, the revelation bounded by the ornate frame that Octave has found for it. She does hate her eyes in the painting. She stares at her image with contempt now. Her nipples are too prominent, too red. Her smile is simpering. Her bush is too aggressive. And of course her shoes are horrible, those awful shoes that seem too big for her feet.

Octave smiles.

—Are you pleased with it?

—I look stupid.

He laughs.

—Everyone looks stupid. We're all stupid animals, aren't we?

Hilary refuses to pursue it. She tells herself that Octave doesn't understand. Of course he paints all his nudes like this. The vacant eyes, the glowing flesh, the wild colors that keep the canvas swimming in a whirlpool. Octave leans against her. He kisses her cheek and he pats her buttocks through her dress and he says she looks lovely in the painting. He says it's a pity it's a frontal nude. He says in the next painting he plans to show more of her derrière.

—More substance, Octave says. More of the true substance.

A week later he has the painting hanging in a new show in the rue Jacob.

The title amuses Hilary: Madame X.

A woman of mystery, Hilary thinks. She stands in the crowd in the gallery. Octave Boulu is always treated with respect, isn't he? The patrons gape at one painting after the other, at Hilary's portrait that hangs over two meters high in the center of the wall.

Hilary takes a seat in an armchair and she watches them. Is she recognized? Do they know that Madame X is sitting here not ten feet from where they stand? She hears the comments in the midst of the gaping. Another shocking nude by Boulu. Four people discuss whether the woman in the painting is an amateur or a professional model. The people continue walking, rouged women on the arms of prosperous looking gentlemen. The lips of the

women are so red. Some of the people are drinking
champagne. Hilary sits in the armchair and she looks
right and left and she begins to be bored by it all. She
wonders if anyone will buy Octave's painting of her. She
wishes now that he'd painted her lying down on that
chaise in his studio. She'd certainly be more appealing
than standing there so awkwardly with her hands at her
sides and her eyes with that stupid look in them. She's
angry now that she allowed Octave to paint her like that.
I ought to have protested. Well, you didn't, did you? And
he has those drawings of her with her legs wide apart to
bring the little hairy rabbit out of its hiding place.

—Hilary, darling.

Vita has appeared. The blonde smiles at Hilary, takes
Hilary's hand as Hilary stands to greet her.

—I was hoping you'd come. I don't know anyone here.

Vita laughs.

—But you know Octave.

—You're teasing.

—It's you in that painting, isn't it? It's marvelous, darling. It's quite marvelous.

—I'm sorry now I agreed to it.

—Don't be silly, it's quite marvelous.

Vita shows her amusement at the painting. Vita's
eyelids are painted blue. A stranger passes the painting
and comments about the model's breasts. Hilary hears a
buzzing sound in her head and she makes an effort to
gather herself together. Yes, she's pleased after all. You
do like the attention, don't you? She wonders how many
of the men find the painting sexually arousing. She
thinks of them as stallions, a herd of stallions prancing
and snorting around the portrait. Walter would be furi-
ous, wouldn't he? All these stallions and their mares.

Now Jan approaches and Hilary introduces him to Vita.
Jan tilts his head as he smiles at Hilary's blonde friend.
Hilary remembers Jan's penis in her mouth. She pushes

the memory back into the shadows as she accepts a glass of champagne from a passing waiter. Sip the champagne, Hilary. The colors in the room seem to undulate now. Octave's colors on the walls. The wild colors quivering and moving in an endless undulation.

Octave arrives and he leads Hilary away.

—I want you to meet someone.

They pass an empty chair upon which one of the guests has placed a full glass of champagne.

These people are wretched, Hilary thinks.

Octave leads her to a tall woman who stands near a Greek pedestal.

—Nora, you must meet Hilary.

So it's Nora Gale, is it? The tall brunette smiles and extends her hand and Hilary takes it.

Nora holds Hilary's hand.

—It's always nice to meet another American in Paris.

Hilary finds Nora's eyes disturbing. Hilary turns her face away. Well, what's the idea of it? She knows it's me in that painting.

Octave is amused.

Or is it something else? What does Octave know of these things?

Nora smiles at Octave.

—She's lovely, darling. I'm quite envious.

Nora gazes at Hilary again.

Hilary suddenly understands Nora's eyes and Hilary blushes.

*　*　*

In Octave's studio, Hilary is still dressed, bent forward over the back of an armchair, her face turned up, her hands grasping the arms of the chair, her buttocks exposed and naked, her thighs partly covered by the brown stockings that are still draw tight⁴ by her long suspenders.

The sun has long gone, only a grey sky visible through the skylight. The room is lit by a pair of electric lamps that throw their light off a blank wall. Two stiff white collars lie on the floor near Hilary, the two collars turned and curving towards each other.

Jan is behind Hilary. He still holds his cravat in one hand, but otherwise he stands naked. He has his organ pushed into Hilary's sex, but he remains motionless, not moving, half the length of his penis visible between the lower curves of Hilary's buttocks.

Octave stands at the large easel, his back to Hilary and Jan, his brush just touching a small canvas, his eyes on a table upon which sits an arrangement of fruit in a black porcelain bowl.

Now Hilary lowers her face and she stares at the purple velvet cushion of the armchair.

Jan moves his left hand, the hand that holds his cravat. He slides the cravat under his testicles and he lifts his testicles against the base of his penis. Then he puts his right hand on Hilary's rear and he moves his hand in a circle over the white skin of Hilary's buttocks. His fingers trail over the rounds of her buttocks, his palm at intervals pressing against the resilient flesh. Then his hand stops moving and he carefully pulls his pelvis backwards to withdraw his penis a bit more from Hilary's sex. He pulls back until only the knob of his organ is still hidden. He moves his left hand again. Once more he rubs his cravat over his swollen testicles.

A shudder passes through Hilary as her sex grips the tip of Jan's organ. The strain of bending over the armchair has brought out the muscles in her thighs and legs. Her eyes are closed again, her mouth open, her lips wet.

Octave has not turned from his easel. He adds a flourish of paint with a small painting knife. He ignores Jan and Hilary. He stands with his legs apart and his eyes on the canvas, then on the fruit, then on the canvas again.

Hilary moans.

The studio has become an arrangement of planes and colors, three people related by a series of lines.

At one vertex is the bowl of fruit, at another Octave and his easel, at a third Jan and Hilary.

Jan is moving again. He keeps his eyes on Hilary's rump as he thrusts himself into her sex, a full thrusting, a pushing forward, a full withdrawal before the next thrust forward.

Hilary stares at the purple cushion of the armchair.

Octave smears a bit of color on the canvas.

Jan continues a slow thrusting, a slow withdrawal and a slow return.

Hilary closes her eyes again.

Jan's cravat is now on the floor and he has both hands on Hilary's buttocks, his fingers extended over the full curves, over the milk-white skin.

Hilary trembles. She moves her legs. Jan stares at the hairy mouth that clutches at his organ. His penis is wet. He touches Hilary's anus with a fingertip. Hilary quivers again. He penetrates Hilary's anus with his right thumb and Hilary shudders.

Hilary closes her eyes.

Then she opens her eyes and once again she stares at the purple cushion of the armchair.

* * *

Sunlight in Hilary's bedroom.

Not a scrap of optimism this morning. It's such a glorious morning and yet here she is in a pit of despair. She moves closer to the open window. She stands at the open window and she gazes down at the quiet street. She hears a voice from somewhere. Is it the pharmacist at the corner? At the far end of the street stands a kiosk plastered with small signs. Byrrh. Crème Simon. La Bal Negre. Hilary gazes at the cobblestones in the street. My little world, she thinks. She hears the maid working in the kitchen.

My marriage is a disaster.

My marriage is a disaster.

My marriage is a disaster.

Hilary wonders if any of the neighbors in the other houses are looking at her. Is her body exposed? She tells herself she doesn't care. She doesn't care what they think. She feels no sentiment for them. She thinks of her marriage and she feels despair again. She tells herself she deserves sympathy. She slides a hand inside her kimono and she holds one of her breasts as she contemplates her despair.

It's unfair, isn't it?

* * *

Oh, the noise now. They have a large table in an awful cellar in Montparnasse. A dimly lit nightclub. Hordes of women with painted faces. Octave and Jan and four of Octave's friends. Hilary has brought Vita this evening. Vita sits with her eyes glued on Octave. Vita seems so delighted with Octave's chattering.

Hilary wonders if she ought to drink enough to make herself intoxicated. She does want to be drunk these days. She's annoyed at Vita. She tells herself that Vita never shows any hesitation about things. Vita is always so certain of herself.

Octave makes a gesture with his hand.

A trio of girls has now come out on the small stage, half dressed, their breasts shaking as they begin a dance of some kind.

It doesn't matter, Hilary thinks. She doesn't care

anymore and it doesn't matter.

Hilary gazes at the breasts of the girls on the stage. She wonders how much Vita knows about Octave and Jan. And these other women at the table. Octave's friends and their women. Hilary no longer remembers their names. The women showed surprise when they learned she was an American.

Octave now has his arm around Vita's shoulders. Hilary wonders if this is the right time to do something to stop it. Does she want to stop it? You don't want to be jealous, do you, darling? She hates thinking about it. She looks at the stage again, at the legs of the girls, their calves and ankles.

I must persist, Hilary thinks. I won't be demolished.

The crowd applauds as the girls on the stage wag their behinds at the audience. The girls are beaming, pleasure in their faces as they blow kisses at everyone.

Vita smiles at Hilary. She leans forward and she touches Hilary's hand.

—It's great fun, isn't it?

* * *

Octave has them all in his studio, the air close, the walls grimy in the yellow light, the horn of the phonograph bleating an aria from Verdi.

Octave is on his back on the chaise, the upper half of his body hidden by Vita as she straddles him.

Vita's dark blue dress is thrown up to her waist, her buttocks naked, her legs covered to mid-thigh by dark silk stockings. Her shoes lie on the floor near the chaise. The upper part of her dress has been pulled off her shoulders. She has her face turned to the right, her eyes closed, her mouth open, her right arm extended as her right hand clutches an ochre pillow.

Octave's thighs and legs and feet are bare, his organ

penetrating the sex of the blonde, his testicles swollen and
separate, Vita's pink nether-lips stretched around the girth
of his penis, her buttocks a curved expanse of white skin,
her anus a pink whorl above the shaft of Octave's organ.

Octave has his hands on Vita's buttocks. Only his left
forearm is visible, but the arm is covered by the sleeve of
his shirt.

Octave's friend Gabriel is with the girl Juliette. Gabriel
is still dressed, but Juliette is naked. Gabriel sits in one of
the armchairs with his legs spread wide and Juliette is
seated in the space made available by his spread thighs.
Gabriel's left hand completely covers the girl's sex.
Juliette leans forward with her head turned to the side as
she watches Octave and Vita. Gabriel's head is tilted
upwards, his eyes closed and his mouth open.

On the other side of the chaise, Octave's friend Luc
and his girl Maria pay no attention to Octave and Vita.
Both Luc and Maria are naked. Luc stands with his hands
lifted to cover his chest and his head bent as he watches
Maria suck his penis. The dark-haired girl is kneeling,
her body forward, her hands on her knees, her mouth
stretched by Luc's thick organ.

Hilary looks at nothing but Vita and Octave. She bends
over a small table, her forearms on the table, her right
knee supported by a stool, the calf and the foot raised.
Jan stands behind her and he has just lifted her dress to
uncover her buttocks. Hilary's breasts are already
exposed, the front of her dress pulled down, the shoulder
straps along her arms, her left breast and her left nipple
completely visible, the tip of her right breast hidden by
her right arm.

Hilary looks at nothing but Vita and Octave.

Vita is moving now, her body moving, her mouth open
as she slowly rises and falls on Octave's organ.

Juliette has risen, and she stands a moment with her
back to Gabriel and her eyes still watching Octave and
Vita.

Maria continues to suck Luc's penis, her mouth moving with a regular rhythm back and forth along the length of his organ.

Juliette leaves Luc and she approaches Hilary.

Jan is gone. Hilary suddenly finds herself alone with Juliette. Hilary stands, straightens her body, her eyes still on Octave and Vita as Juliette slips an arm around Hilary's waist.

Hilary turns to gaze at Juliette, at Juliette's red lips, at the necklace of red beads around Juliette's throat.

Juliette leans against Hilary and she kisses Hilary's neck.

Hilary shudders as she becomes aware of Juliette's perfume.

Now Juliette is touching Hilary's breasts. Hilary continues looking at Octave and Vita as Juliette's fingers roam over Hilary's bare breasts. Juliette toys with Hilary's nipples. She plays with Hilary's breasts with one hand and she strokes Hilary's buttocks with the other hand. Hilary quivers as she feels Juliette's fingers in the crack between her buttocks. Hilary continues watching Octave and Vita, Octave's penis, Vita's hips as they move up and down, Vita's pink sex sliding over Octave's organ.

Now Gabriel has arrived to join Hilary and Juliette. Hilary no longer remembers his name. Is it Rolland? Jan has joined Luc and Maria. They are all naked, the bodies a blur of pink flesh as Hilary watches them, as she moves her eyes from Octave and Vita to Luc and Jan and Maria, as she quivers under the hands of Juliette and Gabriel.

Vita's mouth is open. Vita groans and cries out as she moves her sex up and down on Octave's penis.

Juliette and Gabriel kiss Hilary's breasts. Hilary feels their fingers in her sex. Juliette's fingers or Gabriel's fingers? Hilary moves her thighs apart. She quivers again. Her mind is in a whirl. She hears whispering now and she closes her eyes.

From where? Hilary thinks.

She quivers as she hears the whispering. Vita cries out again. Hilary looks at Vita, but now Juliette has risen and she presses her mouth against Hilary's mouth and Hilary shudders and closes her eyes again.

* * *

This is in a garden somewhere. Late afternoon. Have we seen this garden before? The man is seated on a small bench. He wears a top hat, a dark jacket, grey trousers, a white carnation in his left lapel. He sits with his shoulders slumped forward and his hands hanging loosely between his open thighs.

Beside the man stands a woman. She stands quite erect, her left hand raised, the fingers pinching a long cigarette holder that contains a lit cigarette. She wears a black evening dress, a strand of large pearls around her throat, long earrings, each earring a dangling cluster of small pearls, the earrings swaying slightly as if the woman has just moved.

—I don't like it, the woman says. I don't like it at all.

—What?

—The Eiffel Tower, of course. All those lights make it look so gaudy. Why did they do it? Does anyone know why they did that?

—It's the Exposition.

—It's horrible.

—The tourists like it.

—I don't like the tourists.

—Well, you'll have enough of them at Deauville.

—Then I'll ignore them. I won't look at them. I won't be bothered with anyone who's not French.

5.

It's the usual crowd under the large awning, the tables jammed one against the other and the two waiters sweating in the afternoon heat as they fly from one end of the sidewalk to the other. Arthur Compton sits alone near the black railing, a folded newspaper in one hand as the other hand turns a spoon in his cup of chocolate.

Hilary appears. She comes in off the rue Bonaparte and Arthur doesn't see her at first, not until she's already there at the table looking down at him.

—Hilary!

—Hello, Arthur.

He rises.

—I thought you might not come.

—Well, I have, haven't I?

She sits down. She sits with Arthur at the small table. He takes her hand. When the waiter appears, Hilary orders a lemonade. Arthur looks at her with the eyes of a conspirator.

—You're ravishing.

—Can you get away?

—Get away?

—From that bank of yours. Can you possibly get away for a week or so?

Arthur stares at her.

—But whatever for?

—I'd like you to take me out of Paris. I need to get away, Arthur. I do need a holiday. I suppose you can tell them your grandmother died in Rome or something.

—Oh dear.

—Please, Arthur. . .
—Well, I'll see what I can do.
—Deauville. Take me to Deauville.

* * *

And so a few days later Hilary lies with Arthur on the
beach at Deauville. Bright colored parasols and sunbath-
ers. She's had a break with Octave. She's determined not
to go back to him. She runs her fingers through the sand.
She looks at the ocean, the people in bathing dress, the
striped tents. The sun is so lovely here, the heat so warm
and comforting. Hilary has decided that she hates Octave.
She lies like a languorous kitten on the wide blanket. She
smiles at Arthur's red face. A child is laughing behind
them. The sky is a perfect blue and Hilary congratulates
herself that she's been clever enough to get away from
Paris for a few days.

I need to look after myself, Hilary thinks. I do need to
look after myself sometimes.

Once again she gazes at the men and women on the
beach. All these pairs. All these couples who seem per-
fectly matched. The men are strutting in their wool bathing suits, strutting as they show the bulge of their genitals. Hilary alternates between amusement and revulsion
each time her eyes are confronted by the bulging of the
male apparatus. And of course some of the women are no
better. The French women seem to enjoy displaying their
breasts and buttocks. They show everything. Nothing is
unknown anymore. The beach is covered by a mass of
pink flesh. The carnal heat wafts up from the beach to
compete with the heat of the sun.

All this desire.

Hilary has a new understanding of things. She's been a
mistress, hasn't she? Everyone in Paris knows that she
and Walter are separated and that she's been Octave

Boulu's mistress.

You're a naughty girl, Hilary.

But she feels a warm excitement. It's not Pawtucket, is it? All the lines of her life seem to converge in Paris. She doesn't understand it. She doesn't pretend to understand it.

—Are you comfortable, Hilary?

—Yes, I think so.

—There's no chance we'll run into Walter, you know. He's gone to London until the end of the month.

—Well, that's nice.

* * *

The room at the hotel is done up in white and pale blue. Arthur has the French windows pulled open and he stands at the railing taking huge gulps of the sea air into his chest.

—Oh, I love the sea, Arthur says. I love the summers we had on the Cape. It's not the same here, is it? I mean we're American and not French. I never think it's useful to pretend that I'm French. Paris is a marvel, of course. But sometimes I get so homesick. Do you ever get homesick, Hilary? I can't wait for the fall. You'll come back with us, won't you? I want to get back again. We'll all go back, won't we? I'd rather have New York than Paris when you come down to it.

Hilary is conscious of what a simpleton he is. Of all of Walter's friends, she always thought Arthur Compton was the most ridiculous. And yet here she is with Arthur in a hotel in Deauville. He's too English, really. He ought to be in India somewhere. He hardly ever talks about Walter. I ought to make him talk, Hilary thinks. If he can talk at all. She's happy they're off the beach now. She's tired of the sun today. She thinks about dinner. She wants to please herself with something.

When Arthur turns from the open window, he sees that
Hilary's breasts are uncovered. He smiles at her and he
mumbles something. He's a bore, isn't he? She doesn't
want his conversation, but she has it anyway. She has his
eyes. Hilary can see the desire in his eyes and she feels a
quiver of annoyance. She turns her eyes away from his
red face.

Arthur approaches the bed with diffidence. He has such
courtesy in his manner. Such a damn New England nobil-
ity. He leans over Hilary and he kisses her cheek. He's a
stranger, Hilary thinks. He's kissing me and he's a complete stranger. Then he lowers his head and he kisses her
nipples. He wants to make love. Hilary already has the
top of her bathing suit down at her waist, and now Arthur
helps her get the suit off her body.

He's talking again, mumbling at her, his face flushed.
Hilary wishes he'd forget the conversation. She can't imagine why he thinks she needs his talk. He's on his knees
beside the bed, his eyes on her belly and his face like a
plump red beet. A beet with a motive, isn't he? Hilary
knows what he wants. She turns her body on the bed and
she opens her legs to him. In a moment Arthur has his
mouth on her sex, his moustache tickling her clitoris, his
tongue working in her slit.

All his women, Hilary thinks. He's told her he does it
to all his women.

He sucks at her cleft. Hilary keeps her eyes closed to
avoid looking at him. She can't bear to look at his red
face, the beads of sweat on his forehead, his carefully
groomed brown hair. She looks instead at the open window, the sky, the edges of the window, the ceiling of the
room.

With his eyes open, Hilary thinks. She knows he's
doing it with his eyes open. She knows that if she looks
down at him she'll find his eyes looking at her. Those
pale blue eyes in the beet red face. It's really too much,

isn't it? He's brought me to Deauville, but it's really too much.

* * *

One afternoon Hilary is on the beach without Arthur. She lies alone on the blanket, her face lifted to the sun as she runs her fingers through the hot sand. She closes her mind against the noises of the people on the beach. She imagines she's alone with her secrets. Ignore the crowd, Hilary thinks. All this babbling around her. It's not the old Deauville she's read about. She doesn't want to look at them. They make her think of growing old. She'd rather have the sun. You don't want the reality, do you, darling?

Then finally Hilary can't bear the sun any longer and she slides under the protection of the umbrella. She feels her bathing suit pulling at her body, the wool against her breasts, against her buttocks, against the slope of her belly. She turns on her back and she lifts one leg. Are they looking at her? Ten feet away on her right is a French family and Hilary is certain the man is looking at her. She wonders what he thinks. She feels his eyes on her thighs. I'm a woman of mystery, Hilary thinks. They have two children, two boys tossing sand at each other. Hilary imagines the husband deals in shares at the Bourse. He brings his family to Deauville to get a change of air. She looks at them now. Hilary looks at the eyes of the husband. It's all the same, Hilary thinks. There's no difference, is there? The two boys are giggling. It's all the same and there's no difference.

Now the mother is scolding the two boys about something. Then she takes the hands of the two boys and she leads them away. The husband stands there in front of their umbrella with his hands on his hips and his eyes on the ocean. Does he imagine he's a Viking? When he turns

to look at Hilary, their eyes meet across the sand. How
absurd, Hilary thinks. She looks away; she stares at the
orange and white stripes of the tent on her left. Only a
few moments pass before the husband approaches and
Hilary hears his voice on her right.

—The beach is crowded, eh?

Hilary looks up at him. His body stands against the sky
and Hilary decides he resembles a bear.

—Yes.

The talk begins. He talks about Deauville. After a
while he crouches down on the sand at her right. Now
she can see more of his face. He says his name is Maurice. His eyes are hungry and Hilary is amused. One must
make a judgment, Hilary thinks. She doesn't mind his
eyes on her body. There's no escape, is there? She's here
on the beach and there's no escape. When he stands
again, she sees the bulge of his genitals in his wool bathing suit.

He looks down at her.

—An arrangement?

—About what?

His eyes on the sea again, he speaks out of the corner
of his mouth.

—Five hundred.

He thinks she's a prostitute. What a lark, Hilary thinks.
She wants to laugh. She says nothing.

The man looks down at her again.

—All right, a thousand. Is that good enough?

—Yes.

The word flies out of her mouth and now it's too late to
pull it back behind her lips.

Now he smiles at her.

—You know how to tease, don't you? You've been
teasing me for an hour and now you've caught me.
Where do we go? Do you have a room here?

The words are drumming around in Hilary's head. She

wavers between amusement and apprehension. Hilary, you're a stupid little girl. No, not a girl. A woman. She's a stupid woman. His eyes are on her body again, the eyes measuring, estimating, anticipating.

—Well? he says. Do you have a room here?

—It's not possible in this hotel.

It's an ancient beach, isn't it? All the years are in the sand.

—All right, I'll arrange something. I know the concierge at the Luxor. You're a foreigner, aren't you? I can tell by your accent that you're a foreigner.

—Yes.

*   *   *

In a room at the Hotel Luxor.

Hilary tries to remember. I've become dazed, she thinks. You're in a daze, darling.

She watches him as he pulls the windows open. The noise of the beach is now in the room and Hilary feels a sudden euphoria. I enjoy it, she thinks. What a lark to play the poule. A transaction of the flesh. One thousand francs. His name is Maurice, isn't it?

She removes her beach jacket and then her bathing suit as Maurice watches her. Does he think she's young? Is it her youth he finds attractive?

He approaches her now. He fondles her breasts and buttocks. He murmurs something, a sound of approval in his throat. Hilary feels old again. She touches him. She runs her right hand over his hairy chest and over his belly and down to the bulge of genitals.

She's a poule, isn't she?

He has a firm erection in his bathing suit. She exposes his organ. It's easy enough to pull the wool aside to free his apparatus.

—I washed in the sea, he says.

Did he? She doesn't care. She sits down on the edge of
the bed to suck his penis. He chuckles as he pushes her
hands away. He pulls at the shoulder straps of his bathing
suit, pulls at the suit and peels it down and steps out of it.

Dark hair on his chest and dark hair on his belly and
dark hair surrounding his organ and his scrotum. The
hairy bourse of the man at the Bourse. Yes, he's like a
bear. A bear with a red penis. The knob a cherry-red
color, a cherry-red fruit that waits for her.

She takes his knob in her mouth and she sucks it.

It's impossible, Hilary thinks. What I'm doing is actually impossible. It isn't possible at all, is it? It's beyond
the realm of possibility. Oh Hilary.

His flesh is warm in her mouth. It's not Walter and it's
not Jack and it's not Arthur and it's not that boy Julien
and it's not Octave. This is the man on the beach, the
husband of that dark little woman with two children. Do
they live in happiness? Whatever the happiness is, it's
now Hilary who has him standing before her. This is
love, isn't it? She has the male organ in her mouth and
it's as much love as anything that goes on between a man
and a woman. I'd like to waltz, Hilary thinks. I'd like to
waltz while my mouth is filled.

She finally pulls her mouth away and she falls back on
the bed on her side. She can't imagine that he wants to
finish in her mouth and in any case she wouldn't allow it.
She lies there with her legs open, one hand on her hip,
her eyes half closed as he casually reviews the expanse of
flesh that she offers him.

—You're a beauty, he says.

What a consolation. His penis bobs like a red baton as
he joins her on the bed. Hilary yields to his arms. She
fondles his organ as he kisses her breasts. At this moment
I'm the only one, she thinks. Maurice pulls his mouth
away from her breasts and he rolls over onto his back.
He wants her to mount him. Does he expect her to

refuse? Hilary does not refuse. She climbs over him, straddles his hips, quivers a moment when she finds his organ already pushing at her sex. Then it's inside her. He strokes her hips as she settles down on it. His penis has completely penetrated her opening. She wonders what to do now. Is she expected to act the proper lady? She begins riding him, moving slowly, raising and lowering her hips as she watches his face below her.

Remain elegant, Hilary thinks. Always remain elegant. She hears her mother use the word. Her mother was always so fond of that word.

Then Hilary remembers Vita riding Octave in Octave's studio. Yes. Vita's eyes closed and her face flushed into a burning pink. What an obsession Octave is.

But this isn't Octave, is it?

Hilary continues moving up and down. She finds it exciting. She hears him talking at her. He wants a conversation while she rides him. He plays with her breasts, his hands raised to hold her breasts and rub her nipples. He smiles at her. He doesn't care that she won't talk to him. Does he want the usual way now? No, he wants her to remain as she is. He holds her hips as the pace quickens. Hilary watches the bouncing of her breasts, the trembling of her nipples. She feels the swelling of the organ in her sex. Maurice lifts his right arm in a gesture of some kind, a salute, a wave at an unknown ghost, his eyes rolling up as his penis begins gushing inside Hilary's receptacle.

A breeze suddenly enters the room and Hilary quivers as she feels the cool air on the small of her back.

* * *

In Paris again, Hilary stares at the stark lines of the buildings as the taxi drives up to her flat. The holiday is finished. Arthur kissed her cheek at the station. He seemed eager to return to his bank. I do love you, he said. He waved at Hilary as the cab pulled away into the traffic stream.

Well, it's the flat again, Hilary thinks.

She's happy to be at home again. I do think this is where I belong. She looks at the bundle of letters she received from the concierge.

A note from Nora Gale. Hilary opens it. An invitation.

You can't forget it, Hilary thinks. You don't want the forgetting, do you?

And a letter from Walter. He wants to have lunch with her. My husband wants to have lunch with me. Well, how nice that is. It's nice, isn't it?

Hilary glances at her image in the hall mirror. She tilts her head to the side. All these appearances. Oh darling.

* * *

Marceline is with a man. They have just entered a room in a hotel in Deauville. The man touches his polka-dot bow-tie and he smiles at Marceline.

—You're a pretty little girl, aren't you?

Marceline laughs.

—Isn't that what you want?

—Show me something.

Marceline gives him a coy look.

—What would you like?

—Surprise me.

Marceline pouts. She wears a summer dress with a low neckline, but the slopes of her breasts are hidden by a bit of white lace. Now she slowly pulls the lace away, pulls the dress away to uncover the small globe of her right breast.

She smiles at him as she rubs her nipple with her forefinger.

—Is this what you want?

The man stares at Marceline's exposed breast.

Outside the open window a band begins playing on the promenade.

Marceline continues toying with her nipple, her fingertip moving back and forth, slowly back and forth, the nipple now erect under the rubbing finger, the breast quivering as the band's tuba blows out another small explosion.

6.

The house in rue Jacob is lavish, the drawing room enormous, the Louis XV furniture the finest available in Paris. Nora Gale sits in her drawing room in the midst of her paintings and statues. She wears a white gown, a flowing white gown that covers every bit of her body down to the tips of her shoes. She smiles at Hilary.

Hilary quivers under the direct gaze of Nora's dark eyes. Hilary feels as though she's in a dream. She has no idea why she's here. Nora's world is not her world. Will she bring me happiness? I ought to go home to Mother, Hilary thinks. I'm obsolete here in Paris. Obsolete and overwhelmed. Hilary struggles. She sits quietly in Nora's Louis XV chair and she struggles.

Now Nora's right hand is moving, the fingers fluttering as the hand moves to her throat, to the necklace of pearls, the four strands of the loveliest pearls.

She has a full red mouth. She nods at Hilary again. She looks down at Hilary's ankles.

Well, I'm still married, Hilary thinks. She folds her hands in her lap. She finds herself dazzled by Nora's white gown.

Nora smiles. Her red lips glisten in the afternoon light that pours in through the large windows. She turns her head to the left and then she looks at Hilary again.

—Well, what are you going to do?

Hilary shakes her head.

—I don't know.

—You ought to divorce him if you're unhappy.

Tea is served, the pretty little maid bustling about them as she arranges the teacups on the tiny side-tables.

—How long have you had them?

—What?

—Those lovely bracelets. I've been admiring them.

The maid leaves. Nora crosses her legs inside the long white gown. She crosses her legs and she moves her hands forward to hold her knees.

—You need to pull yourself together, you know.

Hilary nods. She's aware of Nora's eyes.

—Yes.

—Forgive me. I suppose I shouldn't tell you what to do.

—I don't mind.

Hilary gazes at Nora, at Nora's red mouth.

—It's not a question of right or wrong, Nora says. This is a new age and you need to be aware of your independence.

Nora slides her right hand along the length of her left arm.

—You're lovely, Nora says. You're quite lovely, you know.

—Thank you.

Tea and flirtation.

Nora touches her throat again.

—You must come to my little party this evening. The tenor Cremoni will be here. I think his voice is dreadful, but he seems to be in vogue at the moment. He's agreed to sing something. You'll come this evening, won't you?

* * *

It's one of the chic salons of Paris. An evening at Nora Gale's. A soirée at Nora's.

—Do you remember Aristide?

Hilary wanders among the swans. A violin is playing somewhere. The room seems filled with the red lips of women. Nora's naiads. Hilary feels timid in their presence. Some of them are bedecked with jewels. A flamboyant gown of bordeaux red. Feminine hands flutter over feminine shoulders. And here and there a woman in the dress of a man, a soft face above a man's evening dress. Obviously a woman. One of Nora's amazons. Whatever men there are seem amused by it all.

A man bows in front of Hilary, a man with white hair and a red cravat. He begins talking about the Exposition, the markings on the Eiffel Tower, the riot last week in one of the concert halls. Tout-Paris is here. Hilary feels the eyes upon her. Is she one of Nora's little fawns? The talk is all around her.

—What about your mother? someone says.

The faces are indistinct.

Another man arrives and he kisses Hilary's hand. He stares at her bosom.

—What do you think?

—I'm not sure.

—Better early than too late.

A girl laughs. Hilary holds a glass of champagne in one hand. She watches a man waving his arm, his fingers waving, his watch catching the light of the chandelier, his hair glistening with pomade.

—That's Diargue, you know. He always carries an umbrella.

Many of the women wear short skirts, their legs in rayon or silk, grey legs and brown legs and pink legs. One girl with white legs.

Hilary wanders to one of the open windows and she

looks down at Nora's garden, the Japanese lanterns, the pedestals.

Music again. Hilary raises the champagne glass to her lips. She keeps her mouth at the rim of the glass. Nora said she has pretty hands. Yes, my hands are pretty, Hilary thinks. I have pretty hands, don't I? Is it the beginning of something?

I'm a flower, Hilary thinks. I'm just another flower in Nora's garden.

And these other women? Roses with thorns. Some of them do look devilish. Thorns that catch the flesh and make it bleed.

I want glorious days, Hilary thinks. I don't want the scorn of this crowd. She imagines Nora's touch, the sliding of Nora's fingers, the impulse to mysteries.

How difficult it is.

* * *

—I understand it, Walter says. Hilary, I do understand it.

He has her in a restaurant in the Champs-Elysees, the food cluttering the table, the metal cloches gleaming at them.

—Are you sure, Hilary.

—Yes, I'm sure.

—I think we ought to wait.

They have more wine, the steward stiff as he pours the red into the glasses.

—Such nice weather, Walter says.

Hilary stares at the window, at the traffic on the wide boulevard. Well, it's Paris, isn't it? We're in the midst of a party.

—You look wonderful, Walter says.

—Do you think so?

Two women at a nearby table are smoking cigarettes

after their desserts.

—You promised to be reasonable, Walter says.

Hilary gazes at the diners in the restaurant. All the women have darkened their eyes into black hollows.

—People ought to think about real happiness, Walter says.

Is he using pomade on his hair? Hilary studies Walter's hair and she wonders if he's using a bit of pomade.

—Hilary?

—Yes?

—Do you love me.

—Oh Walter.

—Henry Meade told me you came around to his little office. He's very impressed with you and he wants you to work for him.

—I don't think I could manage it.

—It's not a bad magazine, you know. One of the better ones, I think. I'm going to put some money into it. I've been thinking about it and it's really something I want to do. It's a chance to do something. Some of the best poets in the English language are right here in Paris. Henry says that with a little more money he could easily double the circulation.

Hilary thinks of the dust in Henry Meade's office. A dusty little magazine. A magazine filled with dust. When the pages are opened, the dust rises to the sky.

—It's more than an amusement, Walter says.

—I'm sure it is.

—Henry says he'd like your help.

—I don't think I can manage it.

—Well, try it, won't you? If you feel up to it, why not try it?

The two women are looking at them. Walter's voice has carried and the women are looking at them.

They all have their love affairs, Hilary thinks. The women, the men, that little old man with his stiff white collar.

I want to weep. It's such a frightening thing, but I want to weep.

*   *   *

—We're good friends, Vita says.

Her face is turned to the sun. They walk in the Luxembourg, circle the flowerbeds. Vita has such passion in her face. Hilary wants to put her hands on the flowers, but she resists the impulse. Vita smiles at her. Today Vita's mouth is pink more than red. Octave must find it difficult to resist Vita. She has such fine hair.

A child is laughing now, a bubbling little laugh somewhere in the bushes.

—You're not angry, are you, darling?

—No.

—You're not one of those people who get angry about things.

They turn again, another turn around the flowerbeds. The noises of the streets are muted. Hilary looks at the flowers, at the children, at the old women, at the gravel that crunches beneath her shoes.

Am I wrong?

Hilary considers her troubles. She wonders if she ought to be more angry with people. I ought to wish for something. How awful it is. What an exercise in banality it is.

My misfortunes.

My blighted hopes.

Oh God, it's absurd, Hilary thinks.

—I really don't mind about you and Octave, Hilary says.

Vita laughs. She talks about her friends in London. She says she wants them to gossip about her. She waves her fingers at Hilary.

—I need a change, Vita says. I need a change and

Octave is so different.

A man with a red scarf around his throat smiles at them. The path leads them close to the Boulevard St. Michel and now they hear music from the street, one of those gypsy organs, an old melody floating over the bushes and into the ears of the people in the park.

Vita wants to explain. She continues talking about Octave.

—There's a time for everything.

Hilary remembers them, the pink flesh, Vita mounted on Octave like a blonde Godiva on a prostrate horse. Octave's organ so thick in Vita's pink sex.

They pause at a bed of roses.

—Hilary, what are you thinking about?

—Nothing.

—I do love roses.

Hilary feels a sense of excitement. There's no choice, is there? It's not a question of choice. I don't have any choice at all.

* * *

—Oh yes, Nora says.

She has Hilary's breasts uncovered. They sit in the sun-parlor adjacent to the garden, the sun flooding the white walls and the white wicker furniture and Nora's white dressing gown.

Nora murmurs again as she runs her fingertips over the curves of Hilary's breasts.

—Give me your hand.

Hilary extends her hand and Nora lifts the hand to her lips and kisses it.

Hilary trembles.

Nora smiles as she continues to hold Hilary's hand. With her free hand, Nora amuses herself with Hilary's nipples, her fingertips stroking and rubbing and gently pinching until the flesh is turgid and hungry.

It's a virtue, Hilary thinks. No man has ever touched her like this. She feels her body vibrating, a feeling of warmth that flows up and down her spine and out to her breasts.

Now Nora leans forward and she kisses Hilary's mouth. Hilary quivers as she accepts Nora's tongue. What a pleasure it is. She keeps her eyes closed as Nora's mouth continues to press against her own. Nora's hand leaves Hilary's breasts and she runs the hand over Hilary's hair.

It's an advantage, Hilary thinks. It's an advantage to be a woman. Oh yes, it's definitely an advantage.

Nora's mouth is gone. Hilary trembles as Nora drops her head to Hilary's bosom, as Nora's lips close over one of her nipples.

Nora sucks at Hilary's breasts. Hilary groans. She feels more frightened now. She watches Nora's lips as they move from one nipple to the other. The turgid flesh is wet. Hilary's nipples are wet.

Hungry, Hilary thinks. I'm as hungry as she is.

Nora finally pulls her mouth away from Hilary's breasts.

—You're a darling. No, don't cover them. You have such pretty breasts and they shouldn't be covered.

—I feel awkward.

Nora smiles.

—I'm older than you are. My dear, we all feel awkward.

—I don't know what I want. Is that strange? Does anyone know what they want?

—That depends. It's a question of satisfaction, I think.

Nora smiles as she lowers her eyes again to Hilary's breasts. Hilary quivers. She enjoys being looked at. Oh yes, I enjoy it.

—I don't know very much.

—Well, you've got plenty of time to learn.

Then the hands again, Nora's hands touching Hilary's breasts. Two hands this time, the fingers casually caressing Hilary's nipples.

—You need to be patient with me, Hilary says.

—Put your own hands on them. Pretty hands on pretty breasts. You do have pretty hands.

Hilary blushes as she holds her own breasts, as she rubs her own nipples with her fingertips.

—You're ravishing, Nora says. You're quite ravishing.

* * *

They lie naked in Nora's bed, huddled in the privacy, Nora whispering as she strokes Hilary's thighs.

Hilary shudders. Do I want to be seduced? Nora's fingers continue their tickling of Hilary's thighs.

I need a friend, Hilary thinks. I do need a friend.

Then Nora moves, her face moving over Hilary's breasts, her tongue licking at Hilary's nipples. Nora moves again and now her face presses against Hilary's belly.

Yes, Hilary thinks.

She utters a moan as she opens her thighs to Nora's tongue.

Everything is revealed to Nora. The older woman pulls back a bit and she smiles as she looks at Hilary's sex.

How simple it is, Hilary thinks.

She closes her eyes as Nora opens her nether-lips with her fingers.

She trembles again as she feels the first fluttering of Nora's tongue.

Agile, Hilary thinks. She's quite agile. Nora Gale's tongue is quite agile. Hilary has a sudden urge to laugh at the ceiling. Then the urge passes and once again she feels the burning pleasure.

How simple it is.

Then the tongue is gone and Nora's face moves up to Hilary's throat again. A kiss. Nora kisses Hilary's mouth. Nora's face hovers over Hilary. Her fingers play between Hilary's thighs. Hilary feels the fingers probing, penetrating, thrusting.

Oh, the force of it.

Hilary shudders at the pushing force of Nora's fingers.

Nora thrusts again and smiles.

* * *

And another smile in the place Vendome. A room half in shadow, the drapes half closed, the sound muffled by the Oriental carpets. The model stands in front of the round table, one man seated on each side of her, the man on the right adjusting the cuff of her right sleeve, the man on the left adjusting the cuff of her left sleeve, the model tilting her head to the left, her lips pursed, the small black hat hiding her short hair, her right foot thrust forward on the rug in the standard pose of the mannequin.

The man on the model's left wears a white jacket and grey trousers and white spats over his black shoes. He pulls away now, releases the model's wrist as he looks at her.

—Well, that's better.

The other man kneels now to make a final adjustment; then he too pulls back and he sits on his chair again.

—Much better.

—You don't think the hem is too long?

—No, not at all.

The man in the white jacket nods, his eyes on the model's legs.

—Darling, the stockings are loose. We can't have the stockings loose, can we?

The model blushes.

—No, sir.

She lifts her dress to tighten her stockings, to pull at the garters above her knees.

The man in the white jacket chuckles.

—You ought to wear suspenders, darling. The garters are no good for the circulation.

He pinches her left thigh above the top of her stocking.

The model remains motionless, her neck bent, her eyes on her thighs and the pinching fingers.

—Suspenders tomorrow, the other man says.

The model nods.

—Tomorrow, sir.

7.

Lovers now. Hilary has become Nora's lover. As the days pass, Hilary is certain everyone in the world knows it. They all know that Hilary Blair is Nora Gale's new passion. A new flower in Nora's garden. Hilary wonders if she'll find her name in the Tribune. And she's a bitch, of course. Hilary knows that Nora is a bitch. Is that why she finds her so damn attractive? Oh Hilary, you're such a poor little girl, so poor in understanding and so poor in any strength whatsoever.

The nights are sultry. These are the warm Parisian nights when the heart becomes the most important organ in the body. Hilary passes one evening after the other with Nora. Alone with Nora. Or with Nora and her friends. An occasional evening of despair as she finds herself ignored by Nora. Then afterwards hours of lovemaking in Nora's bed.

Such a helpless love, Hilary thinks. I'm so helpless now.

But the pleasure is exquisite. Nora is always precise, the most precise lover of them all. She takes pride in her abilities. Hilary feels that all hope is gone. Her face is on fire.

Then afterwards she's alone again. Afterwards there is nothing but the silence.

I need to be consoled, Hilary thinks. She hears whispering again. Are the voices real or is she imagining them?

Then a smell of flowers. Roses. Lilies. A sweet smell of the flowers in Nora's garden.

Nora is always dominant. Hilary often finds herself mortified by Nora's strength. And her own weakness. How helpless she is against Nora's fingers. Penetrated by Nora's fingers. On occasion Nora seems so cynical about it, her eyes so clear in their statement: I have you.

Hilary's orgasm is always profound. Nora would not allow anything else. The crisis must be total and overwhelming. The room spins as Hilary cries out, as she moans and cries like a helpless fawn.

Nora does not like her sex to be touched. She allows nothing more than a brief stroking of her mound and cleft. No penetration. She will not have Hilary's fingers inside her sex. She does not like to show her breasts. She says her breasts droop too much and she does not like to show them. Often Hilary lies on the bed naked while Nora still wears a white gown that covers her body from her throat to her toes.

—Let me kiss your breasts.

—No, darling.

—Nora, please. . .

—Lie back now and I'll make love to you again.

Hilary always yields. She finds Nora's fingers irresistible. She adores the contact. Two people in a bed; two women. The lamp casts a pink glow over the room. Nora's eyes are so bright when she looks at Hilary's face.

Nora tickles Hilary's thighs with her fingers. Hilary
moves her legs apart. The invitation to the fingers.

—You're exquisite, Nora says.

She has her fingers inside Hilary's sex. Hilary shudders
as the fingers begin a slow movement inside her body.

Completely taken, Hilary thinks. She tells herself she
ought to protest it, protest it at least with her body.

Instead she opens herself.

Nora chuckles as she begins thrusting her fingers inside
Hilary's sex.

—You're drenched, darling.

—Yes.

*　*　*

—I adore women, Nora says. I don't despise men, I
just adore women. They're different, aren't they?

—Yes.

—I adore the skin, the softness, the limbs, the curves
of the soft flesh. Have you seen that Baker woman? She
has the buttocks of a goddess, full buttocks curved like a
pair of brown moons. She's driving the French insane
with lust, you know. It's amusing, isn't it? Kiss me, darling. Don't you want to kiss me?

—Yes.

*　*　*

And Nora's parties.

For Hilary, each moment in the evening is a moment
of revelation. There are people who walk in and out of
the room like smiling ghosts. Nora's lovers. A troupe of
ethereal women. Nora Gale is a high priestess. Hilary
finds herself filled with jealousy, one little jealousy after
another, a succession of twinges, a tightness in the chest.

Does she possess me? Do I want to be possessed?

The rooms are congested with bare shoulders, the

round bare shoulders of ethereal women. Nora can have anyone she likes. Hilary is certain that each of these women have thrown themselves at Nora's feet. Hilary's head swims in the perfumed rooms. What do you expect? she thinks. Hilary, darling, just what do you expect?

They look at Hilary. She has the knowing eyes of the women upon her. Hilary Blair is Nora's new flower. What do they think of her? Hilary feels ashamed of the question. How childish it is. She stands there in the midst of the bare shoulders and she quivers in her shame.

* * *

When the days are quiet, Hilary is often frightened by her attachment to Nora.

I don't know her. Even when we're together, I don't know her.

Hilary hates her own meekness. She hates the way she lies on the cushions half-naked as she waits for Nora. She hates her submission to Nora's strength.

Is it love?

Nora's eyes devour her. Nora smiles as she gazes at Hilary's exposed breasts. Has anything changed?

Hilary shudders as she opens her thighs to Nora's fingers.

—Are you ready for me?

—Yes.

—My little bird.

The fingers are so persuasive. Hilary groans. She opens her thighs even further. She turns her face away to avoid the possession in Nora's eyes. Nora laughs.

—Look at me.

Hilary prays for the darkness.

* * *

Henry Meade sits at his desk with his eyes on Hilary's

throat.

—I'm so glad you've changed your mind.

Hilary smiles. A whim. She does want to be busy. It's a chance to escape Nora, isn't it? Nora has her in the evenings, but Hilary wants the days to be her own.

Henry's eyes are watering as he gazes at her. Hilary can see the watering. She imagines he sees her naked, stripped of her clothes, naked on a bed and waiting for him.

Henry moves in his chair. Is the dust rising again?

—I've never had a female in this office, Henry says. It's always been men, you see. I hope you won't find me difficult. I do need you, you know.

—I'll try to be helpful.

—Walter is a lucky fellow.

Doesn't he know?

Hilary thinks of Nora again. She had all night with Nora and now as she thinks of it she trembles. An entire night with Nora's hand between her legs.

I ought to join a convent, Hilary thinks. I can't go on like this.

Henry is babbling again. What an amusement it is. Hilary does her best to restrain herself. She listens as he talks. She rubs her thighs together and she listens as he talks.

*   *   *

This evening at one of Nora's parties, Hilary meets Ariane.

—My lovely Ariane, Nora says.

Ariane is a countess. Hilary smells Ariane's perfume as Ariane takes her hand. What a beauty she is. Hilary is certain that Ariane is a former lover of Nora's. Yes, of course she is. Nora seems amused as she watches them. Nora is amused as she watches a former lover and new lover together at one of her parties.

Ariane holds Hilary's hand. Ariane has such lovely eyes. Hilary quivers as Ariane gazes at her breasts.

I want to be somewhere else, Hilary thinks. I don't want to be in this place.

But she remains where she is. She remains a prisoner in the crowd. Ariane is flirting with her. Hilary is aware of it, sensitive to the flirtation. Ariane has such white skin, milk-white shoulders. She's more slender than Nora. A difference. Hilary tries to imagine them together. Nora and Ariane. Nora's former lover.

Ariane questions Hilary.

—You have a husband, don't you?

—Yes.

—Nora told me he's not in Paris.

—I think he's in London now.

—Does he travel a great deal?

—Yes.

Hilary does not want to think of Walter. Not here. Not in this place. She thinks of Nora. Last night in Nora's arms again. Nora's fingers in Hilary's sex. The intimacy in Nora's bedroom is always so total. Hilary adores Nora's bed.

Ariane understands. Hilary can see in Ariane's eyes that Ariane understands.

I want to be accepted, Hilary thinks. She's resigned to it now. She realizes that escape is impossible. And now that she understands that, she feels the excitement again.

When Ariane suggests a rendezvous, Hilary accepts.

* * *

A new experience. A new discovery. I want only the truth, Hilary thinks. I want only my own truth.

They sit in a small café near rue Danton. Ariane is smiling. She sips her chocolate and she smiles at Hilary.

—Are you happy?

—I don't know.

—I'll make you happy.

They ride in a taxi to the Florescu house in the rue de Verneuil. Ariane presides in the midst of luxury. Hilary is afraid. I don't want to be afraid, she thinks. She sits with Ariane in the sunlit drawing room as they chat about some of Nora's friends. Ariane insists that Hilary have a glass of champagne with her.

—This is the best time of day for it.

—I don't know if I can manage it.

—But you must try, darling.

Ariane's eyes show her amusement. Hilary wonders about her. She wonders what Ariane requires. Her preferences. There is so much silk in the room, pale blue silk that seems to float around them in a cloud.

Now Ariane leans forward and she kisses Hilary.

—I'm fond of you.

Hilary quivers.

Ariane kisses her again, slides an arm around Hilary's shoulders. She kisses Hilary again and she touches Hilary's breasts. Hilary trembles as she feels Ariane's hand on her breasts. Is it love? Hilary feels the heat in the room, the heat of the sun and the heat of Ariane's hands.

Ariane laughs as she locks the door.

—My maids are quite stupid.

She makes Hilary rise and she undresses Hilary as Hilary stands in the center of a Persian carpet. Ariane smiles with a flush of passion in her face. Hilary stares at the blue silk on the walls as Ariane kisses her again. Must I decide?

Ariane undresses. She has small breasts and narrow hips, a patch of dark fur at the joining of her thighs.

—Over here, darling.

She leads Hilary to a chaise. She kisses Hilary and then

she takes Hilary from behind. Hilary bends on the chaise
to offer her buttocks to Ariane.

—You're an enchantment, Ariane says.

Both places at once. Hilary groans as she feels the
fingers entering both openings, Ariane's fingers entering
and probing and gently thrusting.

Ariane murmurs something. She leans over Hilary's
back and she kisses Hilary's neck. Hilary hangs her head
as she groans again.

* * *

What will become of me?

Hilary sits with Henry Meade in a restaurant. She feels
dull. She thinks of the crazy days and nights with Nora
and now with Ariane de Florescu. Henry is smiling at her
again. He has a nervous twitch on the left side of his
face. He seems so pleased to have her at the table with
him in this little restaurant. What an amusement he is.
Hilary hears his voice as he talks, but she pays no attention to the words. It's an impulse, Hilary thinks. This is
an impulse. Nora was an impulse. Ariane was an impulse.
My marriage was an impulse. My life is an impulse. All
of Paris is an impulse.

Henry is babbling again. His eyes are dancing. In the
office he likes to look at Hilary's legs. Sometimes his face
is so tender. He has the hands of an aesthete. He looks
so fragile as he sits at his lunch. Hilary wonders what
he's imagining. He's mumbling now about buying her a
present. How stupid. He never talks of his wife in England. He never talks of the war. Walter said Henry had a
wound somewhere. I don't want to know, Hilary thinks.
He writes the most awful poetry. She has a continual fear
that one day she'll find a poem about her legs on her
desk. An ode to my legs.

After lunch Hilary walks with Henry. She wishes he

were someone else. But she holds his arm as they walk. He seems pleased. Keep him at bay, Hilary thinks. His pleasure is so ridiculous. Keep the hounds at bay, won't you?

* * *

The Count de Florescu is a distinguished looking gentleman. He smiles at Hilary. He seems to reflect about something. His name is Dimitriu and he has dark eyes. Hilary wonders whether Ariane loves him.

Ariane laughs.

—Americans are very much like children, aren't they?

This evening is unforeseen. Hilary had expected to be alone with Ariane, but now it's evident that Dimitriu will remain with them.

Ariane stokes Hilary's arm. An evening together. Ariane has had pink flowers placed in all the vases in the drawing room.

Dimitriu has a soothing voice. He plays the piano. They have a quiet dinner, the two maids serving them in the candlelight.

Then after dinner they return to the drawing room and Ariane sits beside Hilary on one of the large sofas. They drink champagne again. The servants are dismissed. One of the windows is open and Hilary can see the lights of Paris, the hills of Montmartre.

I do like my comfort, Hilary thinks. She enjoys the calm evenings with Ariane. She's fond of Dimitriu now. Of course he knows everything. He knows what his wife is up to with Hilary. His dark eyes are always untroubled. Hilary often finds him looking at her, his eyes on her legs, her ankles. She enjoys the attention. Ariane seems amused when Dimitriu looks at Hilary.

Hilary is coaxed by Ariane. Whispered words. Hilary is surprised. Then she tells herself no, she has no reason

to be surprised. She had an inkling, didn't she? You know
you did, darling. Why not? Hilary trembles as they leave
the drawing room and walk to the boudoir. Now she feels
the excitement. Her mind is in a whirl as Ariane kisses
her cheek again. Oh yes, I'm trembling. Ariane kisses and
fondles Hilary. She strokes Hilary's breasts. Hilary
vibrates between bewilderment and excitement as Ariane
undresses her. Dimitriu's eyes are burning now, his eyes
hot as he watches them.

When Hilary is undressed, Ariane removes her clothes
in turn. They fall onto the bed, onto the silk counterpane.

Then silence.

A rustling of the silk as Ariane moves over Hilary.

Dimitriu watches them. He holds a cigarette now. The
smoke curls to the ceiling as he watches them.

Hilary lies motionless. She has a sudden moment of
complete confusion. She finds herself unable to recognize
the room. Is this Nora's room? No, darling, it's Ariane's
bedroom. Now Hilary recognizes the smell of incense.

Ariane takes Hilary with her fingers. Hilary is used to
it, of course, but this is the first time anyone has ever
watched it. Hilary kneels on the bed and Ariane takes
Hilary from behind with her long fingers.

Hilary moans. Oh, the pleasure of it.

And the fear. She has such fear of it now. She has such
a complete fear of it.

* * *

It can't be. It can't go on.

In the morning in her flat Hilary is packing. She avoids
looking at herself in the tilted mirror above the bureau.
She wants no awareness of her own image. She flies out
of the flat. A taxi to the Gare Saint-Lazare.

One of the dead, Hilary thinks. The war is finished, but

now I'm one of the dead. She trembles in the rear of the cab as the driver curses the traffic.

It's madness, isn't it?

I have no intention.

They arrive. She pays the driver. Inside the crowded station, she wanders like a blind woman. Her mind whirls. She sees nothing but confusion in front of her eyes.

—Madame?

—What?

—Do you want a ticket, madame?

Then a sign appears, white letters on a black background: Deauville.

Oh, the letters are so white.

—Yes, I'd like a ticket to Deauville, please.

* * *

Three women, a long table covered with embroidered cloth, one woman standing, her lower lip jutting, her body covered with a dark cape. Seated at the table: two women wearing tight dresses, large breasts, large earrings, heavy lip rouge, one brunette and the other blonde, both past forty.

The standing woman is young. She stands far enough forward so that the other women are behind her back.

—No one comes here anymore, the standing woman says. We'll go crazy, won't we? If no one comes any more, we'll go crazy.

She moves her arms and the cape slips off her shoulders and down to the floor.

Above the waist, the standing woman is now nude; trembling gourd-shaped breasts, thick nipples erect and reddened with rouge.

The two seated women, at the same moment and with precisely the same motion, adjust the curls at their temples.

The standing woman cups a hand beneath each breast and she smiles.

—I'd like that sheik in Morocco, that's what I'd like. He'd bring me dates, eh? Would you like that? Don't you like Moroccan dates?

The older women laugh.

—Dates or figs?

—Figs! I'd rather have figs!

PART THREE

Tout-Deauville

1.

Twenty-two people in this room. The roulette table is more or less in the center of the room, the focus of attention, the hub of the gathering.

The croupier is seen leaning forward, his left elbow on his left knee, his right hand extended towards the wheel.

And behind the croupier are a group of bare-shouldered women standing close to each other, pressed against each other as they look at the table.

All the women in the room have bare backs, some of them milk-white, but the others a light golden brown, the skin tanned by the sun, tanned and smooth under the light of the two chandeliers that hang from the high ceiling.

The men are in evening dress, a bit stiff in their starched white collars, more of them with white faces than tanned faces, some of the older men pale white, bald, their noses pink above their white moustaches.

On the left is seated a woman talking to a standing man. This man also has a moustache, but he is younger than the others, not more than thirty, his moustache brown, his body at ease in his evening dress.

Hilary stands behind a seated woman to the left of the croupier.

Hilary has her eyes on the roulette wheel. Her left hand is at her hip. She wears a lowcut Venetian red gown that shows the upper part of her bosom. Her lips are red, but the red is a deeper red, more like a carmine red.

Hilary moves now. She runs the tip of her tongue over her red lips and she looks around her. She looks at the crowd, at the bare shoulders of the women, the men, and then she turns and she looks at the table again.

The croupier moves. He rolls the ivory ball between his fingers.

Then the people around the table move. They shift their bodies and gaze at the croupier's hand, at the ivory ball, at the wheel on the table.

Hilary hesitates. She never knows whether to place her chips now or to wait until the wheel is spinning. She hates the waiting. She leans over the table and she places the four chips on red, on the diamond.

The people are staring at the table as if they expect an appearance of some kind.

The croupier's hand touches the cross-handle and suddenly the wheel is spinning.

The croupier's fingers toss the ivory ball onto the spinning wheel.

Hilary quivers. Well, it's better than Paris, she thinks. It's much better than Paris. She watches the wheel, the ivory ball, the spinning cross-handle. She loves the wonder of it. The magic of the spinning wheel. She watches the bouncing ball. Everyone around the table is watching the bouncing ball.

They don't know me, Hilary thinks. And I don't recognize anyone, do I?

The ball falls in and the wheel slows to a stop.

The number is black.

*   *   *

In the morning Hilary walks alone on the beach. She passes the striped chairs. She thinks of Walter again. Has he returned to Paris? The striped chairs and the striped tents run parallel to the sea along the entire length of the beach. Hilary wears a thin cotton shirt, thin white cotton that shows the shape of her breasts. In Paris she wouldn't dare walk like this in the street. Here it doesn't seem to matter. The women show the curves of their breasts, the shadows of their nipples, their thighs and buttocks.

The sea is lovely. Oh, I do like the sea, Hilary thinks. She adores nature. Now she thinks of the note she sent to Henry Meade from the station in Paris. Will he think she's mad?

The birds are circling. Hilary wonders how high they can fly. Every living thing has its limit. She thinks of her mother. Her mother would be horrified, wouldn't she? Oh yes. Hilary shudders as she glances again at the blue sky. My mother is not a woman who fancies pleasure. Her mother would not understand Ariane.

Now Hilary stops and she slips her sandals off her feet. She walks again, this time barefooted on the white beach, her feet bare on the wet sand near the rolling surf.

Some of the women are out now, preparing their morning exposure to the sun, rubbing their shoulders and arms with lotion.

Well, it's a question of money, Hilary thinks. If you have enough money you can have whatever you want.

She lifts her head again. She likes the feel of the sun on her face. She passes the women and she doesn't mind the way they look at her.

I don't mind it. I really don't mind it.

*   *   *

At eight o'clock in the evening Hilary is gambling again. This time she sits at the roulette table. She sits at the right of the croupier with a new pile of chips in front of her. My folly, she thinks. She's using up whatever money she has. But there's excitement in it. She feels the excitement in her spine.

The croupier drones on as he prepares the table. Hilary wears a blue dress tonight, a silk dress that clings to her body. Thin shoulder-straps. A décolleté front that shows the rise of her breasts.

The croupier glances at Hilary's breasts before he spins the cross-handle. He tosses the ivory ball. He glances at Hilary again.

Hilary is amused. They're all beggars, aren't they? The men are beggars. The women here are beggars. The wheel spins, the people push forward.

I need remorse, Hilary thinks. I have no remorse for anything. She looks at her chips. She watches the wheel. She places her bet. The others are betting around her, pushing their chips forward. The croupier calls out and the betting stops.

We pay for our sins, don't we? The wheel slows down and the ball falls in. Hilary has lost again. She lights a cigarette. She doesn't care if she loses. She has no tears for the ivory ball.

What you need is a great passion. You need a great passion, darling. A woman without a great passion is nothing but a dead flower.

The croupier's eyes are on Hilary's breasts again. Hilary ignores him. She waits for the wheel to start spinning again.

Four hours of it.

Then an hour of champagne as she stands and watches the play continue at the table.

At one o'clock in the morning, Hilary is drunk in the lobby of the hotel where she has a room.

But the lobby is crowded and she's not noticed.

I'm safe here, Hilary thinks. I might be raped on the beach but I'm safe here. She giggles to herself as she imagines an attack in the moonlight. She sits down in one of the chairs in the lobby. Are they whispering about her? The chandeliers are so huge. The walls are lavishly decorated, the patterns weaving in front of Hilary's eyes. She closes her eyes and then she opens them again.

Hilary, you're potted.

She stands and she walks. Carefully now, the carpets

•

are so deep.

Well, this is life, isn't it? Yes, the people are looking at her. She suddenly feels naked in her brief little dress. They can see everything she has. She stumbles. You're not bold enough, she thinks. Hilary, darling, you're not bold enough. These are bold people and you're just not bold enough. Her long necklace swings back and forth as she moves from side to side.

The concierge suddenly appears. He smiles at Hilary.

—Let me help you, madame.

Hilary avoids his eyes. He's a jackal. They're all jackals, aren't they? She wants to dance. Would they mind if she did a dance of some kind?

—Let me help you, madame.

He's not a jackal, he's a vulture; he feeds on dead flesh.

She takes his arm. She holds his arm as he guides her across the lobby.

The carpets are really too deep, aren't they?

* * *

The promenade in the afternoon. Hilary wears a new sunhat and she walks. She loves the sea air. One can't live without these ephemeral pleasures. The breeze is delicious. The shops are so elegant.

I want revenge, Hilary thinks. I want to avenge myself.

Her skin tingles in the sun as she walks. She enters a parfumerie. This is Deauville, and the woman who smiles at Hilary takes a measure of Hilary to guess if she carries a royal title.

It doesn't matter: Hilary pays an exhorbitant price for a small bottle of something. She feels happy as she walks on the promenade again.

More women now. They walk in pairs or threes, a great many hats, some with parasols, a slowly moving display of thighs and buttocks.

In another shop, Hilary buys an alligator purse. What great fun it is to count out the franc notes and then laugh when she offers too many. Does the clerk wonder about her husband? My husband is somewhere between London and Paris. Hilary thinks of all the beds in Deauville and she wonders how many are empty of husbands.

She buys a pair of lapis luzuli earrings, frightfully expensive, the blue stones hanging like teardrops from her ears.

I'm just a caricature, Hilary thinks. Really, just a caricature. American woman on the promenade at Deauville. These men at the rail who stand and smoke as they look at her. They want to be groaning at her. All these groaning men.

Hilary continues walking. She feels the heat now, the burning of the sun. She holds her packages. The earrings are lovely. She does like the earrings. She thinks of Walter again. Has he told his family anything? Hilary wonders what they will say about it. Everything turns to ashes, doesn't it? That's my history. Walter's father is an ogre. It's not possible to have any sort of communion with that man. He has such dead eyes. Hilary shudders as she thinks of the dead eyes of Walter's father. The wedding was horrible, wasn't it? She had such fear when she met them the first time. She hates Boston. All those dry lips. And then that silly honeymoon in the Bahamas. They decided to avoid Europe because they knew Walter would be transferred soon to Paris. Men are such fools, aren't they? Walter was so delighted with her virginity. Fumbling in the dark. She remembers her contempt afterwards. Fury and contempt. She hated the darkness. What a futility it is. One dreams of beauty and the reward is futility and sweat and despair. But of course her mother would understand that, wouldn't she? Her mother always said futility is the essence of marriage. Hilary has the

memories. She thinks of the house again. Dear Mother,
what would you say about my recent days in Paris? Do
you understand my ecstasies? Shall I cut my hair again?
And what of her friends in Pawtucket? It seems so silly to
be here in Deauville and to think of Pawtucket. I want to
know everything. There, that man is smiling at me, isn't
he? Does he know the dreams? We all have our dreams,
don't we? Dreams of childhood, Hilary thinks. She
remembers a place in the wood near the house, the trees
thick enough to hide the sun. A smell of spring in the air
in April. She was never that virtuous. She had her
games. She loved flowers. She loved a festival of any
kind. She wanted nothing but years and years of happiness. She did not want these tears. Dear God, I did not
want these tears.

*   *   *

And of course in the evening Hilary gambles again.
Now she sits on the right of the croupier, and if she looks
at the large mirror on the far wall she often has a glimpse
of herself.

She wears the lapis lazuli earrings.

The spinning wheel has become an obsession.

Losing continuously. Mrs. Hilary Blair seated at the
table and losing continuously.

I need angels, Hilary thinks. She finds it amusing.
She's losing enormous amounts of money. All the money
Walter set aside for her. But it doesn't matter because
she's quite certain she'll win it all back. In the meantime
she'll have her fun. Better Deauville than Paris. She
wonders what they see in her eyes. Do they see any
tenderness? Do your eyes show tenderness, Hilary?
What an amusement it is. Her arms are bare. The woman
beside her sighs as the ball falls into a slot again.

Again and again.

Hilary is always aware of the eyes of the men. She enjoys the eyes, the questioning in the eyes. They've never seen her with a man. Do they think she's a widow? That's amusing, isn't it?

The ivory ball is falling again.

The cross-handle of the wheel is a crucifix.

Walter would be horrified, wouldn't he?

The croupier drones on, his head turning slowly, his fingers moving. Hilary decides the croupier is a phantom. She wonders if he can see her nipples. She quivers as she thinks of all the money she's lost.

* * *

At midnight, in the lobby of the casino, Hilary sees an old man who has been a spectator at the roulette table night after night. An old addict. He wears proper evening dress, but the suit is certainly not new. He nods at Hilary. She looks at his face and she sees the hell in his eyes. He's on the edge. He has a fever in his eyes. They stand there and they gaze at each other. Now his eyes begin to radiate gratitude.

Hilary smiles.

—I'll take you to supper, she says.

The old man stares at her.

—What?

—I said I'll take you to supper. You haven't had supper yet, have you? Come along with me.

She takes his arm and she leads him to the restaurant adjacent to the casino. It's absurd. The old man keeps mumbling as they follow the headwaiter to a table. Hilary orders the wine. What great fun it is.

She smiles at the old man.

—What's your name?

He coughs.

—Dauzat, madame. Jules Dauzat.

—You can call me Hilaire.

—Madame is very beautiful.

The amusement continues. Hilary enjoys his eyes, the eyes of the other diners. Monsieur Dauzat seems cultivated. He holds his left arm in an awkward position and she wonders if he was wounded in the war. She wonders if he can smell her perfume. His hands are so expressive.

Monsieur Dauzat starts mumbling again. He talks of Monte Carlo. He says Monte Carlo is much more pleasant than Deauville.

—More distinguished.

Hilary nods.

—Yes, I suppose so.

You must have courage, Hilary thinks. In the face of futility, one must have courage.

—Would you like more wine, Monsieur Dauzat? I'll order another bottle. •

* * *

This is not particularly clear: a street of stone steps behind the casino, badly worn, chipped, covered with grime, seven steps and beyond that a passage of cobblestones, down on the first step a seated woman leaning against the wall of an old building.

The woman is dressed in black, black stockings and black shoes with high pointed heels. Her hands are folded in her lap. Her face is raised and the back of her head rests on the wall. Her eyes are lowered but not closed, her glance directed somewhere to the side, to her right side.

Up the steps again on the cobblestones: a small fountain or a marker of some sort, a coat of arms chiseled into the stone. Now a man appears beside the fountain. He wears a black coat, a white shirt, a tie, a pair of new black shoes. He has a long thin face. He extends his hand to the fountain, touches it, moves the back of his hand to his lips. He walks down the steps and he stops at the last one, the first step, the step at one end of which the woman is sitting with her back against the old wall.

The man looks down at the woman and he puts his hands inside the pockets of his jacket.

—Today is Wednesday, the man says.

The woman sighs. She does not look at the man. She continues to glance somewhere to the side, her eyes lowered. Then she unfolds her hands and her right hand begins to pull the hem of her dress back along her thighs. The hand stops moving when the tops of her black stockings are uncovered.

The man looks down at the exposed skin of the woman's thighs. Suddenly he turns and he walks up the steps to the fountain, extends his hand to the fountain, touches it, moves the back of his hand to his lips. And then he turns and again he walks down the steps and he stops at the last step, the first step, the step on which the woman is sitting. The man looks down at the white skin of the woman's thighs; he looks at her face, he nods, he extends his hand to the woman.

The woman sighs again. She takes the man's hand and she slowly rises until she stands beside him on the first step.

2.

After a week the money is gone. Hilary has nothing. So many thousands of francs vanished into the casino and the shops. She still has the desire to gamble, but now there is no money for it. She thinks of all the money she's lost. How does she defend it? What defense do you have?

Is it two hundred thousand francs? The hotel concierge is now glancing with suspicion at Hilary. The bill will soon be presented to Madame Hilary Blair. Her marriage still has some significance here. She thinks of Walter again. Oh, what a boy he is. He ought to come here and spend night after night with her at the casino. He might grow up if he did that. Hilary thinks of home. What nostalgia. Well, she can't possibly approach Walter now. What she has now is desperation. At this moment it's a question only of desperation. Always despair, isn't it? I always have the desperation of a woman. My womanly despair. It's an amusement, isn't it? Do you want happiness, Hilary? Deauville is one temptation after another. Well, you must use cunning now. What you need now is an order of protection. A bit of cunning, little darling. Wipe away the tears of frustration and pull yourself together. You can't delay things any longer, can you? The time has come to wipe the tears away.

In the morning, in the white hotel room, Hilary turns in her bed. How late is it? She has the dreams in her head. She rises finally. She takes the path to the bathroom first. Then she pulls the French doors open and she steps out on the small balcony.

Are you afraid, Hilary? I don't care, really I don't. The sea in the morning is a thing of beauty, isn't it? Oh, I do love the sea.

She's not dressed. She wears only a miniscule silk chemise that hardly covers her body. If anyone on the beach would look up at the terrace, they would certainly see her secrets.

It must be late. The beach is already crowded with bodies. Hilary looks down at the people with amusement. If I had a lover, we could both jump off the balcony and become immortal.

Don't be silly, darling. People from Pawtucket do not jump off balconies in foreign lands.

The sun is hot. Hilary decides that later she'll have a walk on the promenade again. She turns from the balcony now and she enters the room. How lovely it is to be alone. She's not like some other women: She enjoys the freedom. You don't mind it, do you, Hilary? She pulls the chemise off her body and she walks naked in the room. She stands before the full-length mirror and she studies her breasts and her belly and her sex. The dark little bush at the joining of her thighs. Her little rabbit, Octave called it. Your life, he says. It's the source of a woman's life. Hilary grimaces at herself in the mirror. A woman's life and a woman's death. You mustn't approach Walter. You must not ask Walter for any money. You're not a fool, are you, darling? You don't want to be a fool.

* * *

After lunch Hilary walks along the promenade. She wears a white dress, the skirt blown around her knees by the breeze. She feels happy in the sun. As she passes the open gallery of a restaurant, she hears music. A violin? How lovely. She passes the people standing at the rail, the strollers who gaze at her. She imagines the curiosity in their eyes.

I don't feel blue, Hilary thinks. I don't want to feel blue. A person needs to be aware of the joys in life. Life is joyous, isn't it?

She wants to laugh but she has the eyes of people upon her. She's not wearing much of anything under her dress and she wonders if they can guess it. The men undress me; the women assess me. I don't care. It's a mad life, darling. Poor little Hilary has such a bag of troubles. You don't want to cry, do you? Think of the war, darling. Think of all those dead soldiers.

Well, damn the war. I don't want to think of the war.

The women on the promenade are looking at her.

Hilary suddenly remembers Ariane and Nora. It doesn't mean anything; you were always drunk when you did it with them.

Hilary swings her purse as she walks. Do I want oblivion? The sun is too glorious for that. The sun is much too glorious.

—Hilary?

A voice.

Hilary stops, turns, freezes.

Dear God, it's Henry Meade.

His eyes are wide as he looks at her. He stands alone at the rail. He's been looking at the beach and now he's looking at Hilary.

—What a surprise, Henry says. What a happy surprise.

Hilary quivers. My salvation. After all the gloom, the sky is blue again.

* * *

She takes him to one of the cafés. Hilary is amused because she feels the thrill of it in her sex. How ridiculous to feel that with Henry Meade.

He's in Deauville with his wife.

—Which hotel?

—The Normandie.

—I'm at the Royal.

—I didn't know what to think when I got your note.

He touches her hand. Hilary smiles. What a delight. His eyes are so happy. Oh, you're a scheming bitch, Hilary. She's amused at herself. Something new, darling? Never before? She touches his arm with her fingers. Yes, he's blushing. Hilary smiles as Henry blushes. Does he realize she knows?

—Henry, can you possibly lend me some money?

—Money?

—Five hundred dollars. I seem to have run out.

—Five hundred dollars?

—That's a hundred pounds, isn't it?

He's not blushing now. He rolls his eyes at her. Hilary is suddenly afraid, but she pushes the fear out of her mind and she touches his arm again.

He's a man of merit, isn't he?

—Hilary, where's Walter?

—We've separated.

—Oh dear.

—Please, Henry, I do need the money.

—You know I'm not a rich man.

—Surely, you have that much.

He sits back in his chair. He stares at her. Hilary sees him with more lucidity now. His cheeks are so pink. Is it a blush or is it merely the sun on his English skin?

—I'll let you sleep with me, Hilary says.

—What?

—If you lend me the money, I'll let you sleep with me. You do want that, don't you?

—Hilary, you don't mean that.

—Yes I do. I do mean it, Henry. Isn't that a fair bargain? Don't you want to?

Uncertainty in his eyes.

Then his lips move.

*   *   *

She thought she might get the money and arrange a rendezvous in a day or so. But no, he wants the consummation immediately. He says his wife is always with him and it's only today that he has a few hours on his own.

Oh, he's hungry, all right. Hilary can see the hunger in his eyes.

Five hundred dollars, Hilary.

She takes him to her room at the Royal.

She opens the French windows. Like that Frenchman

with two children, she thinks. She can't remember his name. Was it Maurice? Well, this isn't Maurice, it's Henry Meade.

Hilary turns and she smiles at Henry. He sits ill at ease in a chair near the bed. He stares at her as if he suspects she might change her mind.

But of course she won't change her mind.

I ought to wear a long gown, Hilary thinks. A long sacrificial gown of flowing silk.

Henry has such wanting in his eyes. Hilary feels amused again as she sits down near Henry. It's a mystery, isn't it? All that wanting. His excitement. The male quivering in his need to put that rod of flesh into the female. She can't imagine what it will be like with Henry Meade. She can't imagine his organ pushing inside her body.

She teases him. She takes one of his cigarettes and she gets him to talk about Deauville. He mumbles at her, his eyes on her body, her legs, the soft white dress that covers her thighs.

He says he's known his wife since she was a girl. They have a small house in the West End.

Hilary enjoys it. It's a play, isn't it? She needs to remember her lines, that's all. Just do the lines, darling. She smiles at Henry as she unbuttons the front of her dress. She pulls the dress off her shoulders, and then she rises and she slips out of the dress altogether.

Henry stares at her. She wears nothing but a thin chemise. No underwear. Hilary pulls at the shoulder-straps of the chemise and in a moment her breasts are uncovered.

She sits down again.

The upper part of her body is bare, the chemise still covering her belly and thighs.

Henry's face is flushed. He trembles slightly as he gazes at her breasts.

—Am I worth five hundred dollars?

—Oh yes.

Hilary looks down at her breasts, at her pink nipples. When she was a girl, she was always amazed by her breasts. She always thought her breasts had such promise.

Now she feels the madness of it. This is Henry Meade staring at her. She's the wife of Walter Blair and this is Henry Meade staring at her in Deauville.

—Do you want to see more of me?

He makes a sound in his throat.

—Yes.

Hilary pulls at the chemise, lifts it and then pulls it up and over her head and arms.

She opens her legs to show Henry her sex.

She takes pleasure in it. Oh yes, I do like it. She enjoys showing herself to him. She enjoys the look of hunger in his eyes, that lovely hunger that makes her feel so completely secure.

—And now you, Henry. We can't do anything while you're still wearing your clothes. You're not coming into my bed with your clothes on.

Henry trembles as he undresses. The trembling is apparent. He still seems uncertain about what's happening. Will the verdict be life or death? Hilary is amused. She teases him again. She goes to him and she kisses him as he undresses. She helps him. He seems so helpless now and she wants to comfort him. He's like a baby, she thinks. Then she tells herself that she's absurd to think that. Henry Meade is not a baby. She thought the same of Arthur Compton, didn't she?

Henry is undressed, his lean white body naked in the airy room, his penis pink and quivering and quite stiff.

Hilary closes her hand around his organ. No chastity. This is not the moment for chastity. She feels the heat of his penis in her hand. He's not that old. He still has the vigor of youth.

The lines, darling. Do remember your lines, will you?

She sits down in the chair again and she leans forward to take his penis in her mouth.

Henry shudders.

Hilary sucks his organ. She looks up at him once, at his florid face. Then she looks at the open window, the sky, the small white clouds.

Henry shudders again as she rolls her tongue over his knob.

—Aren't you happy now?

—Yes.

When they finally go to the bed, she lies down on her back with her legs dangling over the edge of the mattress.

—You can do what you want, Henry.

The pleasure is in his face, the pleasure and hunger and the heat of his excitement.

He sits on the edge of the bed and he touches her. He runs his fingers over her throat and shoulders. Hilary wonders if he's afraid of her. He touches her breasts. She feels his fingertips tickling her nipples. She closes her eyes. Does she feel any desire for it? Just the beginning of something. In her belly. Henry's fingers are moving again. He strokes her belly. He touches the little bush that covers her mound.

The altar, Hilary thinks. That's the altar they all want to pray at.

She opens her legs to Henry's fingers. He's more adept than she expected. His fingers aren't clumsy at all. He opens her sex with a degree of skill. Stroking fingers.

How many years ago was it that Walter was the only lover she'd known?

Four months?

Now Henry kneels on the floor at the side of the bed and he opens her thighs to get his mouth on her sex.

Hilary rubs her eyes. She amuses herself by recalling the others, the other mouths, the other faces.

Nora Gale was undoubtedly the best. Hilary quivers as she thinks of Nora. She quivers under Henry's mouth. He has her sex now. He has her completely. He's more aggressive, more forceful. He behaves like a man possessed by a demon. He sucks at her sex like a starved animal. Hilary shudders in response. She holds his head with both hands now. Henry's tongue rasps over her clitoris again and again. Hilary squirms on the mattress. She lifts her head, cranes her neck to watch him. When he pulls back a bit, she can see his tongue so pink and wet in her groove.

The tongue is a mirror, Hilary thinks. Nora said that. Then Hilary groans as she feels Henry's tongue tickling her anus. That too.

He wants her there. When he pulls away and tells her to roll over, she knows what he wants. He shows no uncertainty now. She's a tart now. Hilary imagines he's had them in London and he's had them in Paris. She does what he wants. She rolls over on her belly to offer him her buttocks. He fondles the cheeks of her bottom. She has the knowledge of it. She had it often enough with Octave. And now it's Henry's turn. It's what he wants. He mumbles at her. Hilary guesses he always buggers his tarts. She feels him leaning against her. She feels his organ pushing between her buttocks, pushing at the secret place, at the little bud, at the dark opening, pushing in, thrusting forward, Henry groaning.

Hilary is vanquished.

Groan, you bloody bastard, groan at me.

* * *

Brilliant sun, dark shadows, a long flight of stone steps leading up from the beach. Two women dressed in black slowly climb the steps, slowly, their heads bowed, the older woman plump, plump legs in black cotton

stockings, her hands at her waist holding a rosary, the
younger woman slender, a black dress that shows her
knees, black silk stockings, black shoes with pointed
heels, her right hand holding a black purse, the purse
near the right kneecap.

The women climbing, the legs moving, the legs slowly
climbing the old stone steps.

3.

Henry's money pays for another week in Deauville.
Hilary is happy again. In the morning she lies in bed
thinking about Henry; then in the afternoon she walks on
the promenade again. The evenings are always devoted to
the casino, watching the wheel, the betting, the ivory ball.

She sees no more of Henry: he leaves Deauville
immediately with his wife. He flees from Hilary.

He's afraid of me, Hilary thinks. She wonders what his
wife is like. Then she tells herself she doesn't care. Will
Henry tell Walter what happened to him in Deauville? I
don't care about that either.

How strange it is to see all the idols broken and
smashed. Hilary is amused by all the changes in her life.
She holds her breasts in the morning. She gazes at her
nipples and she feels such tenderness towards them.

I don't care about anything. I don't know myself
anymore.

Is she afraid?

She doesn't know.

In the afternoon in a café a man stares at her. Hilary
imagines herself with him. She imagines herself and the
man together in a room. When he smiles at her, she
smiles back at him. In a moment he rises and he comes to

sit at her table.

His name is Georges and he says he's a Belgian diplomat.

Hilary doesn't care. She tries to imagine him thrusting at her. Eventually the image completes itself and she agrees to go with him to a room in exchange for two thousand francs.

He seems to think the price is quite reasonable.

*   *   *

The Belgian diplomat on Tuesday. An Englishman on Wednesday. A Parisian stockbroker on Thursday.

Between five and seven in the evening, Hilary does a tour of the bars and cafés of the hotels. She enjoys the crowds. She dresses with discretion, her bosom covered, her dress not short enough to be daring. She sits at a table with a glass of lemonade and an ashtray.

Yes, she does like it. It's more real than anything she's known. And exciting. The sexual excitement is always there. The men are surprised to find her wet when they take her.

On Saturday she has two men in one day. Husbands escaping from their wives. One man in the afternoon and one man in the early evening. In her room at the Royal. She has the window open and she lies on the bed listening to the ocean as they make use of her body.

They want her to do this and that. She doesn't mind. She does what they want. This position or that position. She likes it best when she's taken from behind. The coupling has more of an animal intensity and there's no need to look at the man while it's done to her.

It's the animal intensity that the men have. If it's a question of softness, Hilary understands that she prefers women.

The men look at her now when she's at the bar at the

Hotel Royal. The staff knows. They accept her. Sometimes she sees a glance of amusement.

That's fine too. She doesn't mind that either.

* * *

Then one afternoon the concierge of the Royal approaches Hilary in the café. His eyes are heavy and he seems drugged. He offers Hilary a cigarette; he slowly shifts his body in his chair as he gazes at her.

His name is Antoine.

—You seem to be registered with us as Mrs. Walter Blair.

—Yes.

—Will your husband be coming to Deauville soon?

—I don't think so.

—Do you want to register with the police?

—The police?

—Women of a certain kind must register with the police. Do you want that?

Hilary shudders.

—No, of course not.

Antoine smiles.

—That's understandable, isn't it?

Hilary trembles as he gazes at her. She's afraid now. She wonders what he wants. She hadn't thought about the police. She wonders what Antoine has in his mind. Does he want a bribe?

Antoine explains. He wants something more than a bribe. He wants a partnership. A percentage. Thirty percent.

—We can work together, he says. I can put you on to people and it can be quite lucrative for both of us.

Hilary feels a sudden amusement.

Well, you're into it, aren't you, darling?

Thirty percent isn't that much.

Antoine smiles when Hilary agrees. He talks about partnership again. He orders cognac and they drink a small toast to each other.

—You're a beautiful woman.

—Thank you.

—We ought to celebrate our new partnership in the proper way, don't you think?

—Yes, why not?

Hilary is amused as they leave the café together. She's to go to her room and wait for him. Well, it's a business arrangement, Hilary thinks. Antoine is certain that he can provide the sort of client she wants, the rich men in Deauville who might be interested in an attractive American woman.

Then she has Antoine with her. It's five o'clock and the beginning of a pleasant evening at the seaside. He's not a bad sort. Hilary wonders if she ought to change her room. She's tired of these walls.

Antoine exposes his penis and he wants her to suck it.

—I don't have time for anything more complicated. It's a pity, isn't it?

She sits on the edge of the bed and she takes his knob in her mouth.

I like it, Hilary thinks. It's more of life than she's ever had. She feels the pulsing of his flesh between her lips. She sucks with pleasure at his stiff organ. She wonders if Antoine has a mistress. Then she reminds herself it's only a business arrangement.

Antoine suddenly pulls away.

—You need to be more skillful.

—What?

He gives instructions. Hilary stares at him as he talks about the proper way to suck a penis. He moves his hands as he talks. Then he pushes his penis at her mouth again. His organ visits her mouth as he continues talking.

Hilary learns.

She feels victorious when she hears Antoine make a sound of pleasure. She enjoys the primitive strength she has. She feels his passion and she enjoys it.

He spurts in her mouth. He groans. Hilary sucks at the fountain as Antoine shudders.

* * *

There is no difficulty now. Antoine makes the arrangements. They agree that Hilary will have no more than two clients during any one evening. The money is quite enough and she's content with it. Her life is now more unreal than ever. She feels as though she's entered a magic wonderland, a fantasy of some kind acted out on the edge of the sea.

The days and nights are warm and lovely. The casino is more entrancing than ever.

One evening Antoine sends Hilary an Argentinian, a dark-eyed aristocrat already noticed by Hilary in the casino.

Señor Paroli complains that his life in Argentina was banal. He says he's tired of living blindly. He opens a small leather case and he hands a short black whip to Hilary.

He lies on the bed naked, on his belly, his white buttocks like a pair of moons.

All the veils are removed.

Hilary holds the black whip in her hand.

Does he really want it?

Señor Paroli says yes.

Hilary does what he wants.

Voluptuous sensations course through her body as she whips those white buttocks.

She doesn't mind it. She enjoys it. It's a violation of all her sensibilities, but she does enjoy it.

What an amusement it is.

Señor Paroli does want it.

His orgasm is intense. Hilary watches the shuddering, the shuddering Argentinian on her bed, the frenzied groaning as he spends on the counterpane.

* * *

On the beach again. Hilary hardly ever thinks of home now. She turns on her belly to avoid the glare of the sun. This is nearly the end of August and the crowd is not as dense as it was. The men and women on the beach seem sanctified by the hot sun. They want to be browned by the sun. They show their bodies. The myth of modesty is absent here. Hilary feels so languorous. She adores the comfort of the beach, the physical pleasure of feeling her body warmed by the sun and cooled by the air. She doesn't look at anyone anymore. She doesn't care. She has her afternoons and evenings. Antoine, after all, is a man of some delicacy. Hilary is amazed at how much she enjoys her liaisons.

My new métier.

The men are so vulnerable, aren't they? The penis is rigid and the man is vulnerable.

Her face resting on her folded arms, Hilary quivers as she closes her eyes again.

* * *

Tonight Antoine proposes a special rendezvous at the Hotel Royal. Monsieur and Madame Barrault.

—They've seen you at the casino. They're quite taken with you and they're paying double.

Hilary is not pleased.

—I've never done it that way.

Antoine smiles.

—You've never been with a woman?

—Not for money.

But it's all the same, isn't it? Antoine convinces her and Hilary finally agrees. Hilary wonders who they are. The name means nothing to her. When she arrives at the Barrault suite, it's the wife who opens the door.

Madame Barrault smiles.

—Ah yes, please come in. We've been waiting for you. We haven't opened the champagne yet.

Monsieur and Madame. Monsieur Barrault is a tall man with a serene face. Madame Barrault is more nervous, her dark eyes always on Hilary, the eyes measuring and hungry.

Hilary decides she doesn't know them. She doesn't remember them at the casino. What does it matter?

The husband pours the champagne. What do they seek? What does anyone seek here?

Madame Barrault smiles at her husband.

—Why don't you fondle her? Don't you want her?

The husband touches Hilary. He uncovers Hilary's breasts and he kisses her nipples. The wife's eyes are burning as she watches it.

—She has pretty breasts, doesn't she?

The wife touches Hilary's breasts. Hilary quivers under the woman's fingertips.

They have more champagne. The husband and wife chat as they move about the room. Hilary remains with her breasts uncovered. Then the husband puts down his champagne and he returns to Hilary. He runs a hand over Hilary's buttocks. He squeezes her buttocks through the silk of her dress.

—Do you like her? the husband says.

The wife laughs.

—But of course I like her. It was my idea, wasn't it?

The husband lifts Hilary's dress to look at her legs, at the tops of her stockings and her garters, at her long thighs.

The window is open and the cool night air is in the

room. Hilary quivers as she feels the cool air on her thighs.

The wife stares at Hilary's legs.

—Don't you want her to be naked? We ought to have her on the bed naked.

In a few moments Hilary lies naked on the bed with her sex exposed to their eyes.

Are the women always more savage than the men?

Her face flushed, the wife pounces on Hilary, pushes Hilary's knees up and then drops her mouth down to Hilary's gaping sex.

The husband moves behind his wife and he lifts her dress to fondle her buttocks. He pulls her panties down. He drops his trousers and his drawers and he calmly inserts his penis in his wife's anus.

The wife groans against Hilary's sex and she sucks Hilary with more vigor.

Hilary is detached from it now. It's too much. It's much too crazy and she doesn't want to understand it. She keeps her legs pulled back to her breasts. She enjoys the wife's tongue, but she doesn't want to think about the husband.

They have their dreams, don't they? Hilary tells herself they have their dreams. She quivers on the mattress as the husband continues thrusting at his wife.

The wife is skillful, her tongue delicious on Hilary's clitoris.

I'm still innocent, Hilary thinks. I don't know anything. I don't know anything at all, do I?

Hilary cries out as she has her climax.

The wife sucks hard at Hilary's clitoris and Hilary's orgasm becomes endless.

* * *

Near the Hotel Normandie in Deauville is a place

called the Café Verte. Hilary likes to sit there in the afternoon with a newspaper and a cup of chocolate. The season is coming to a close now and the café is filled with many of the cheaper girls who parade on the promenade in the evening. These girls will soon return to Paris and new opportunities, but in the meantime they congregate at the Café Verte and laugh together as they tell each other stores of their adventures.

Hilary notices a pretty girl who sits alone at an adjacent table. The girl is young, dark-haired, extremely attractive. She has a heart-shaped face and red lips. The girls looks at Hilary occasionally and she smiles.

What does she want?

Hilary reads her newspaper.

The noise and the smoke in the café are more annoying today than ever before.

Hilary looks at the girl again.

Oh dear, Hilary thinks.

She feels an interest. The more she thinks of the interest, the quicker the interest becomes a desire.

Was it Madame Barrault who started this again?

Hilary's eyes meet the girl's and they smile at each other.

In a short while the girl is sitting at Hilary's table.

—I've seen you on the beach, the girl says. And at the Royal bar. It's a rotten life, isn't it? It's all right for the pigs with money, but for us it's a rotten life.

Hilary's desire for the girl is sudden and intense. The girl is exquisite, fragile and feminine and as tempting as a delicate confection.

Well, what is it? Hilary thinks. Is it just an amusement? No, it's not just an amusement. I want her. I do want her. Oh yes, I do want her.

—You're lovely, Hilary says.

—Thank you.

—My name is Hilary.

The girl smiles.

—And my name is Marceline.

* * *

A group on the beach. Six women are dancing in a ring around a man in the center. They are all in bathing dress, all of the women wearing bathing caps, one of the women wearing black shoes with high heels, the other women and the man in the center wearing beach sandals.

The ring moves.

The women are laughing.

The man is laughing.

The game is called Kiss in the Ring.

4.

They lie exhausted on the bed, motionless, Hilary lying on her side with her head raised and supported by her right hand as she looks at Marceline's face.

Hilary is in love with Marceline.

The first, Hilary thinks. My first true love.

Hilary quivers as she thinks of it. Yes, she does love Marceline. She adores the girl. She adores Marceline's face, her eyes, her mouth, her breasts, her belly, her sex.

A shudder of delight passes through Hilary. She feels confronted by a force unknown to her before. She glances down at the tuft of dark hair that covers Marceline's sex. The girl's breasts are lovely, her nipples delicious red points.

I know a great secret, Hilary thinks. I know the secret of a great love. She knows the wonder of it. She knows the happiness.

Hilary leans forward and she kisses Marceline again.

Marceline murmurs against Hilary's lips. Marceline slips
an arm around Hilary's neck. The girl sighs.

—I love you, Marceline says.

—And I love you. You're my treasure.

Marceline giggles.

—I don't know any Americans.

—I'm the only one you need to know.

Hilary kisses her again, their mouths fused, their
tongues meeting in a fluttering duet.

Hilary strokes the girl's breasts. She playfully pinches
Marceline's hard little nipples. Then her hand moves
down over Marceline's belly to her dark-haired sex. A
full sex. The lips are ripe and full and swollen under
Hilary's fingertips.

Marceline stirs. She moves from side to side on the
mattress. Her eyes are closed, her mouth open, her face
flushed.

Hilary is thrilled. The girl adores being taken by
Hilary's fingers. Marceline is shuddering now as Hilary
strokes her clitoris, her bud, the quivering point of passion.

She's mine, Hilary thinks. The girl belongs to her now
and the idea of it causes a tremendous excitement in
Hilary. She trembles with the need to possess Marceline.
She leans over the girl, her fingers still stroking
Marceline's clitoris.

Then Hilary's fingers open the girl's sex. She pushes
her fingers inside, a slow penetration, a slow possession.

Marceline groans as Hilary takes her.

Hilary quivers at the mystery of it.

It's an adventure, Hilary thinks. She's had nothing like
this before. Not this passion she feels, this tender love.
There was none of this with Ariane or Nora. And certainly none of it with any man.

Hilary's fingers are thrusting now. Marceline moans,
raises her knees, covers her eyes with a forearm.

—Is it good, darling?

Marceline cries out.

—I love you!

I want her in Paris, Hilary thinks. She keeps her fingers thrusting in Marceline's sex. Hilary thinks of Marceline in Paris as she watches the girl finish her climax.

Afterwards, Hilary rolls over on her back and Marceline moves on top of her. Marceline giggles as she kisses Hilary's neck, as she kisses and sucks at Hilary's breasts.

I want her in Paris, Hilary thinks. I want her in a boudoir and not just this hotel room.

Hilary folds her arms around Marceline. She holds her prize in her arms. She kisses Marceline's face. She's unhappy that she's not the girl's first woman. Marceline has already admitted that she's had other women in Paris.

—Tell me about the first one, Hilary says.

—The first one?

—Your first woman. Who was she?

Marceline smiles.

—The woman who runs the first house where I worked. Madame Mathilde.

—Mathilde?

—Yes, Mathilde. Madame Mathilde.

—In rue Rossini?

Marceline laughs.

—Yes, in rue Rossini. Do you know her?

—Yes, I do know her.

Hilary controls her annoyance. She can't bear to think of Madame Mathilde and Marceline together. It's not possible to think of it.

Then Marceline is kissing Hilary's thighs and Hilary tells herself to forget Madame Mathilde. She's mine now. Marceline is hers and Madame Mathilde is nothing but a memory.

When Marceline wants to put her fingers deep inside

Hilary's sex, Hilary refuses.

—No, darling.

—You never allow me to do it.

—Not that.

Marceline pouts. But she knows what Hilary wants and she likes that even better. In a moment the girl has her mouth on Hilary's sex. Hilary groans as she opens her thighs to Marceline. The room spins in front of Hilary's eyes. She trembles as Marceline sucks her clitoris. Dear God, what a caress that is. Marceline is such an expert. Hilary closes her hands over her own breasts and she squeezes them with happiness. Marceline continues the sucking and soon Hilary throws her head back as she cries out to the ceiling.

* * *

Antoine is annoyed.

—You spend too much time with her.

—That's none of your business.

—We have an arrangement.

—Yes, but I'm not your mistress. It's just a partnership.

Is he annoyed because Hilary's lover is a woman? Is he annoyed because he thinks Marceline is too cheap for the Hotel Royal?

Hilary is still much in demand. Antoine says the men have been asking for her.

—You're a great success here.

Hilary doesn't care. All she cares about now is her love for Marceline. She doesn't care about the men and the money they give her.

But of course she does need the money.

—Marceline is going to move in with me.

Antoine fumes.

—That's absurd.

—Absurd or not, that's the way it is.

—Will you still be available?

Hilary assures him the men can still have her. Antoine knows the money is important to her. It's a compromise. He pulls at his moustache as he looks at her. He sighs. He nods. All right, you can have what you want.

* * *

Marceline moves into the Hotel Royal to live with Hilary.

Hilary is happy. She has Marceline. On the promenade she and Marceline are always seen together and people know them as a couple. Before long even Antoine is happy about it. Hilary continues to be available in the evening and Antoine is satisfied with the new arrangement. Now he's more pleasant to Marceline. He jokes with the women and he buys them presents. When he hints that he might be interested in an hour or two with both Hilary and Marceline, Hilary refuses.

—She's not for that.

—She was on the promenade, wasn't she?

—I said she's not for that.

—What a pity.

Then he talks about Hilary's rendezvous for the evening. An Indian prince. She's to wear her best jewelry.

—Preferably pearls, Antoine says.

—But why?

—I don't know. His secretary says he prefers pearls.

Hilary buys five strands of fake pearls. She doesn't mind the idiocies now. She's in love. She spends her afternoons with Marceline in the cafés and on the beach. Hilary will not allow Marceline to return to the promenade as a poule. No more of that. Marceline belongs to Hilary and Hilary will not allow it.

Marceline is amused.

—I don't mind. I don't like it that much.

—All your time is for me.

—Yes.

They kiss each other with affection. Hilary leads Marceline back to their room and they make love again with the window open to the breeze from the sea. Later Hilary makes Marceline try on the new clothes that Hilary has bought for her.

She's like a wife, Hilary thinks. Marceline is her wife, a pretty little wife with firm breasts and firm buttocks.

Oh, I do love her.

* * *

—Will you stay with me in Paris?

Marceline smiles.

—Will you be a poule in Paris?

Hilary quivers.

—I don't know.

—Do you have a flat?

—Near the Luxembourg. Darling, you must live with me. We'll have a lovely time, won't we? We'll go to London in December.

—I don't want to go to London.

—Then where would you like to go?

—I don't know. Maybe to Monte Carlo.

—All right, we'll go to Monte Carlo.

—I'll need new clothes.

—We'll go shopping as soon as we return to Paris.

—A large hat. I want a large yellow hat to wear in Monte Carlo.

—Then you'll have it. We'll find the prettiest hat in Paris.

—Do you have maids in the flat in Paris?

—Maids? Yes of course. Two maids.

Marceline touches one of Hilary's nipples.

—I think I'm going to like living with you in Paris.
—Yes, darling, yes.

* * *

Now the bleating of a saxophone on the empty board-walk. It's the last of Deauville, the last of the season.

Hilary holds Marceline in her arms.

It doesn't matter, Hilary thinks. Nothing matters, does it? Nothing matters except this. Nothing matters except a dear true love, a dearest true love.

Marceline murmurs.

—I'm sleepy.

Hilary smiles and kisses her eyes.

The saxophone bleats again, a more protracted note, a long bleating over the promenade and over the white sand and over the empty tents on the Deauville beach.

The women hold each other in the fading light.

Available now

SHADOW LANE

In a small New England village, four spirited young women explore the romance of discipline with their lovers. Laura's husband is handsome but terribly strict, leaving her no choice but to rebel. Damaris is a very bad girl until detective Flagg takes her in hand. Susan simultaneously begins her freshman year at college and her odyssey in the scene with two charming older men. Marguerite can't decide whether to remain dreamily submissive or become a goddess.

———————

Available now

SHADOW LANE II
Return to Random Point

All Susan Ross ever wanted was a handsome and masterful lover who would turn her over his knee now and then without trying to control her life. She ends up with three of them in this second installment of the ongoing chronicle of romantic discipline, set in a village on Cape Cod.

———————

Available now

SHADOW LANE III
The Romance of Discipline

Mischievous Susan Ross, now at Vassar, continues to exasperate Anthony Newton, while pursuing other dominant men. Heroically proportioned Michael Flagg proves capable but bossy, while handsome Marcus Gower has one too many demands. Dominating her girlfriend Diana brings Susan unexpected satisfaction, but playing top is work and so she turns her submissive over to the boys. Susan then inspires her adoring servant Dennis to revolt against his own submissive nature and turn his young mistress over his knee.

SHADOW LANE IV
The Chronicles of Random Point

Ever since the fifties, spanking has been practiced for the pleasure of adults in Random Point. The present era finds Hugo Sands at the center of its scene. Formerly a stern and imperious dom, his persistent love for Laura has all but civilized him. But instead of enchanting his favorite submissive, Hugo's sudden tameness has the opposite effect on Laura, who breaks every rule of their relationship to get him to behave like the strict martinet she once knew and loved. Meanwhile ivy league brat Susan Ross selects Sherman Cooper as the proper dominant to give her naughty friend Diana Stratton to and all the girls of Random Point conspire to rescue a delightful submissive from a cruel master.

SHADOW LANE V
The Spanking Persuasion

When Patricia's addiction to luxury necessitates a rescue from Hugo Sands, repayment is exacted in the form of discipline from one of the world's most implacable masters. Carter compels Aurora to give up her professional B&D lifestyle, not wholly through the use of a hairbrush. Marguerite takes a no-nonsense young husband, with predictable results. Sloan finds the girl of his dreams is more like the brat of his nightmares. Portia pushes Monty quite beyond control in trying to prove he's a switch. The stories are interconnected and share a theme: bad girls get spanked!

Order These Selected Blue Moon Titles

Souvenirs From a Boarding School $7.95	Shades of Singapore $7.95
The Captive $7.95	Images of Ironwood $7.95
Ironwood Revisited $7.95	What Love $7.95
Sundancer $7.95	Sabine $7.95
Julia $7.95	An English Education $7.95
The Captive II $7.95	The Encounter $7.95
Shadow Lane $7.95	Tutor's Bride $7.95
Belle Sauvage $7.95	A Brief Education $7.95
Shadow Lane III $7.95	Love Lessons $7.95
My Secret Life $9.95	Shogun's Agent $7.95
Our Scene $7.95	The Sign of the Scorpion $7.95
Chrysanthemum, Rose & the Samurai $7.95	Women of Gion $7.95
Captive V $7.95	Mariska I $7.95
Bombay Bound $7.95	Secret Talents $7.95
Sadopaideia $7.95	Beatrice $7.95
The New Story of O $7.95	S&M: The Last Taboo $8.95
Shadow Lane IV $7.95	"Frank" & I $7.95
Beauty in the Birch $7.95	Lament $7.95
Laura $7.95	The Boudoir $7.95
The Reckoning $7.95	The Bitch Witch $7.95
Ironwood Continued $7.95	Story of O $5.95
In a Mist $7.95	Romance of Lust $9.95
The Prussian Girls $7.95	Ironwood $7.95
Blue Velvet $7.95	Virtue's Rewards $5.95
Shadow Lane V $7.95	The Correct Sadist $7.95
Deep South $7.95	The New Olympia Reader $15.95

Visit our website at www.bluemoonbooks.com

ORDER FORM
Attach a separate sheet for additional titles.

Title	Quantity	Price
_____	___	_____
_____	___	_____
_____	___	_____
_____	___	_____

Shipping and Handling (see charges below) _____

Sales tax (in CA and NY) _____

Total _____

Name _____

Address _____

City _____ State _____ Zip _____

Daytime telephone number _____

❏ Check   ❏ Money Order   (US dollars only. No COD orders accepted.)

Credit Card # _____ Exp. Date _____

❏ MC   ❏ VISA   ❏ AMEX

Signature _____

(if paying with a credit card you must sign this form.)

Shipping and Handling charges:*

Domestic: $4 for 1st book, $.75 each additional book. International: $5 for 1st book, $1 each additional book
*rates in effect at time of publication. Subject to Change.

Mail order to Publishers Group West, Attention: Order Dept., 1700 Fourth St., Berkeley, CA 94710, or fax to (510) 528-3444.

PLEASE ALLOW 4-6 WEEKS FOR DELIVERY. ALL ORDERS SHIP VIA 4TH CLASS MAIL.

Look for Blue Moon Books at your favorite local bookseller or from your favorite online bookseller.